倍斯特出版事業有限公司
Best Publishing Ltd.

一次就考到

雅思寫作

論點具可信度且總是驚艷考官

韋爾 ◎ 著

7+

MP3

三大學習特色 精選圖表題高分字彙／規劃作文段落拓展
／收錄暢銷書論點

掌握圖表題高階字彙：巧妙運用圖表題高階字彙於小作文中，提升對**「字彙掌握度」**的分數，拉高寫作的整體得分。

納入作文段落拓展：協助基礎考生**邏輯式組織段落文句**，縮短構思作文時間，高效提升應考時的臨場反應力。

搭配暢銷書論點：鞏固本身立場或提出的論點，提升文章的**說服力**和**可信度**，具體化文句的表達。

Editor's preface

作者序

　　雅思寫作考試，包含了圖表題小作文和大作文，小作文要求要寫出總字數至少 150 字的英文文章，而大作文的部份則需要寫至少 250 字左右的作文。要獲取更高的成績，小作文的部分考生大概需要 180-200 字，而大作文則大概要寫出將近 300 字。（書中收錄的大作文長度約為 400-450 字，更充分提供考生更多的論述點。）這比起指考英文作文對考生的要求多出了非常多，在一小時中要手寫出近 480 字英文，是沒有太多時間去構思的，要如何寫這兩類型的作文，考生先要要求自己能把在腦海中想到的想法等以英文思考，即刻就寫出這些想法且是英文文法正確的句子。再加上，考官給分是相當嚴格的，字數有少的話，則在寫作任務的要求那欄是會被扣分的。

　　從劍橋雅思近幾年的考官點評中可以看出，考官願意給雅思寫作 7 分的成績，代表考生是沒有什麼文法錯誤且文筆流暢的。而考官能給到寫作 7.5 的分數，考生寫的文句除了通順，在用字等方面，都用到了常見的高階字彙等等（詳見劍橋雅思 14）。在圖表題的部分，考官給 6.5 的寫作分數，或許對考生來說會覺得有點過於嚴苛，認為自己都有將重點論述到，那麼問題點到底在哪裡呢？我一直覺得這是一個很好的問題，因為蠻多英語程度好的考生確實考了數次，但都是獲得 6.5 的成績，好像中了魔咒，無法突破這個門檻，去詢問考到寫作高分的考生，對方也說不出個所以然，某部分也造成了有些考生開始衝高「聽力」和「閱讀」單項的成績，拉高自己的雅思平均成績。想要獲取寫作高分其實是有跡可循的，例如：語句的表達太過單一，則不可能獲得太高分的分數。例如一篇簡單不過的曲線圖配有各個年份（像是書中的圖表題中關於棕熊族群變化的圖），考生可能除了開頭的描述句，都使用了「in+年份」為開頭，去描述變化，像是 In 1990, there was a steady increase...。書中的曲線題範文總字數共 209 字英文，其中只有一句是這樣的開頭，其他都以各種形式句型來替換，避免在表達過於單調。（這僅僅是其中一點關於考生未能於考試中獲取寫作高於 6.5 分的其中一個原因。）

　　還有像是在圓餅圖等圖形描述中，考生可能覺得每個要點都描述到了，但很重要的一個部分考生缺少了。列出每個重點是很詳盡沒錯，卻缺少了各個重點的相似處或相異處之間的比較，這部分更是考官看中的重點。除此之外，圓餅圖和其他圖表題的難度也在增加，例如在劍橋雅思 14 Test 1 就包含了三個圓餅圖在一張圖形的出題。考生可以抓住這點，更多的圖形代表有更多的重點可以用於進行比較，各個重點的比較和搭配邏輯性的表達，就能跟一般的考生範文做出區隔並一次性考取雅思寫作 7 以上的成績。

　　除了圓餅圖的備考外，考生太喜歡或擅長答線條圖或條狀圖，但是在答像是地圖題或流程圖題卻看到題目時一時之間反應不過來了。（雅思考試四個單項都非常重要，遇到不擅長的圖表題時，許多考生就會因為寫作分數的拉低而必須要重新考試。）某部分是為了要更能檢測出考生的程度，除了劍橋雅思反應出的題型變化，在實際考試中「**地圖題**」確實有增加的趨勢，考生還是必需要熟悉各式的地圖題型跟流程圖題。沒有充分準備一時之間真的會不知道要寫什麼，像是腦海中想到，「以順時針方向來看...這張圖」，可能會面臨想的到要如何描述，但英文寫不出來的困境。書中對於地圖題強化的部分，納入了雙地圖題，（雙地圖題在劍橋雅思 13 和 14 中均有收錄，不單單只是一張地圖，而是兩個地圖），考生會需要綜合兩張圖的資訊來描述。熟悉地圖題的考生也要注意失分的情況。地圖題充滿許多需要注意的點，像是「**時間點**」，第一張地圖題標示的年代是 2017 年的話，時態上就必須要使用過去式，表達過去的狀態，所以答這類題型還包含了在時態上的掌握度。書中的雙地圖題則是表示過去和未來的兩張地圖。此外，書中還納入了雙金字塔圖題和流程圖題，考生可以學習高分回答（畢竟在流程圖和地圖題中要拿到高分，確實比起答線條圖和圓餅圖等難）

　　書中收錄了精選字彙並且圖文呈現，考生只要熟悉很少量圖表題的字彙就能獲取 7 分以上的成績。（在小作文中約使用 6-7 個）**靈活使用是個很大的關鍵**，例如很多考生都會造像是 there was a decrease/increase...in 1999，想要拿高分還遠遠不夠。考生必須掌握更多部分才能獲取高分（不能僅是造句），例如 ❶ 熟悉 decrease 跟反義詞 increase 在圖表題的用法、❷ 能靈活使用 decrease 和 increase 在各圖表題中當**動詞**和**名詞**的用法且以正確的時態在各語句中表達出、❸ 能搭配像是 dramatic 的形容詞，而成了 a dramatic decrease（但如果要獲取高分，這些還是遠遠不夠的，a dramatic decrease 仍然太模糊了）、❹ 搭配像書中介紹的高階形容詞（不用記很多）且把敘述具體化，例如改成 a **staggering 50%** decrease（這樣比起考到寫作 6-6.5 的考生**更具體**的表達了增幅或減幅到底是多少，但還是不夠）❺ 學習高階圖表題動詞，像是使用 **balloon**（激增），（高階動詞是可以取代這樣的描述且前方還可以用更高階的副詞修飾，如此還可以修改成更佳的描述）❻ 使用高階動詞後搭配同位語表達（例如：使用高階動詞描述完後加上同位語 a staggering 150% increase from last year，語句會更豐富，**variety** 是能否獲取高分的關鍵）❼ 搭配其他句型，除了 ❶-❼ 還有很多強化點（非常建議背書中的曲線圖和其他圖形的範文並熟悉書中介紹的所有字彙），書中的精選字彙雖然才介紹 24 個字，但是其實很浩瀚，真的能**靈活使用**圖表題字彙並搭配句型，就能獲取高分。

最後要說明的是雅思寫作大作文，除了澳洲打工的建議那一篇，所有篇章都搭配了暢銷書論點強化，讓作文更有內容（有內容是能否獲取高分的關鍵），也能提供考生很多思考點，這能讓考生表現的更獨一無二並獲取高分。書籍中的範文均有音檔，能迅速提升考生臨場撰寫文句的能力，不過還是要注意要融入自己的想法，以自己的體驗來回答（**避免被考官評定為抄襲**）。大作文的部份就請考生細細品味，各個主題包含許多切入點、句型和想法，這些都能用於類似或不同主題的雅思大作文考試中。最後祝考生在短時間備考後就能獲取理想成績，脫離雅思魔海。

韋爾 敬上

Instructions 使│用│說│明

Part 1 雅思寫作 Task1 精選高分字彙

【 halve 將…對分，減半/腰斬 】
- As a country heavily reliant on the import of the ingredients, the higher price for raw materials has made the number of products nearly halve in the first quarter.
身為高度仰賴原料進口的國家，較高

Halve

額的原物料價格已經導致產品的數量在第一季時腰斬了。

【還能怎麼說】
- Due to the economic downturn, the payment for all executives in the company almost halved during the second quarter.
由於經濟蕭條，所有公司的高階主管的收入在第二季營運期間幾乎砍半。
- Since profits from illegal hunting for marine creatures nearly halved in the last year, no one wants to invest more money in the company.
既然海洋生物非法盜獵的利潤在去年近乎砍半，沒有人想要在投資更多金錢再這間公司上。

〜 小提點 〜

Halve 的同義詞有 divide, dissect, split, share。這個字當動詞的用法可以適時運用在考試中增添表達力。例如前一句表達出數據是以倍數成長但後期數值卻是腰斬，比較不單調。

22

【 nose-dive 價格等的暴跌 】
- Best Airlines reported a 60% nose-dive in its third quarter profit to 25 million dollars.
倍斯特航空公司報告了它在第三季利潤暴跌了 60%來到兩千五百萬元。

Nose-dive

【還能怎麼說】
- Badly injured by the bidding war, the stock price of the Best Airlines took a nose-dive, making the total revenue dip to 4 million dollars.
因為競賽戰而受到嚴重傷害，倍斯特航空公司的股價暴跌，使得整體營收降至四百萬元。
- Because of an 80% nose-dive in the fourth quarter, Best Airlines is unable to win the support from the shareholders.
因為在第四季有著 80%的暴跌，倍斯特航空公司無法得到股東們的支持。

〜 小提點 〜

Nose-dive 這個字彙特別的，也鮮少考生使用，非常建議考生使用，它用於表達「**數值的暴跌**」，也比單純僅使用 a dramatic decrease 好且高階，可以多練習這個字和 **after or before** 一起搭配的句型，在一個數值暴跌之前或之後...，圖形變化為何呢？

23

雅思寫作 Task1 精選高分字彙　雅思寫作 Task2 完整攻略

圖文呈現，精選 24 個高分詞彙
靈活使用，一次就考取雅思寫作 7 以上得分

- 別不信！真的只要 24 個單字就能搞定「圖表題」作文，除了例句外，還另外規劃兩句「**還能怎麼說**」和「**小提點**」強化考生具體表達和靈活使用文句的能力。

「段落拓展」規劃，強化考生組織和邏輯表達英文的能力

- 有效協助大多數考生組織文句、臨場反應和靈活運用句型的能力。
- 詳細解釋高分原因和強化句型 **variety**，拿到試卷就能下筆，省去構思的時間。（上過許多英文寫作課仍無法有效拉高寫作能力者更適用。）

整合能力強化 ③ 段落拓展

TOPIC

The diagram below shows the number of the brown bears from 1949 to 2019. The population encountered several fluctuations due to natural disasters. The statistics conducted here measures the number of brown bears per decade.

Summarize the information by selecting and reporting the main features, and make comparisons where relevant.

Step 1 先看題目的圖表題為何種形式，並統一以 **Given is/ are...diagram(s)**....or **A glance at the graph(s)**....等套句開頭，避免使用 the pic shows...等較低階的簡單句型。
- 在有年份的圖表題時，要避免每句開頭都是 in+年份，這樣會顯得單調，所以次句以 from 1949 **onward** 為開頭。
- 使用更能體現圖表題的專業字彙像是 fluctuation，並加上高階形容詞 consecutive，表示是一接續的波動，另外在天災的描述部分換個字彙，catastrophes。
- 下一句以 It is **intriguing** to note...為開頭，常見考生使用 it is interesting to note。若改用 intriguing 其實更好代表你知道這個較 interesting 高階的字彙。

Unit 2 曲線圖題：棕熊族群數量因為天災產生的波動

- 使用 went through **oscillation** 和 at a ten-year interval，代表族群經歷的擺動和圖表的年份是以 10 年為一個階段。接著描述族群的數量在最開頭和最尾端都是相同的數量，一千隻。

Step 2 接著也是避免使用 in+年份為開頭，改使用 from the onset 為開頭，並描述 there was a slight climb...。接續以高分慣用語 exponential **growth** 描述族群的成長，並搭配高階動詞 balloon（激增）表達出數量在 1969 年達到 6000 隻。

Step 3 接續改以 Then a decade later 開頭，外加高分語彙 **reached a** plateau，表達族群進入高原期，且此情況接續到下個十年。開頭使用 in 1989，搭配用高階字彙 pinnacle 表達族群達到顛峰，以 but 表達轉折接續搭配高階慣用語 did not remain constant，最後接續以高階字彙 plummet 描述族群的下降，此句後搭配使用「同位語」表達這與前年是 a dramatic decrease，最後使用名詞 a mild **reduction** 表達些微的下降，最後用動詞的表達 descend 結束描述的部分。

Step 4 最後總結，使用 succession 和 natural calamities 豐富表達，最後陳述出族群數量在開頭跟結尾維持一致。

Instructions 使│用│說│明

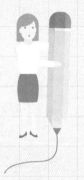

翻譯「中譯英」規劃，用更道地的語句表達

- Task 1 圖表題寫作和 Task 2 大作文均附中譯英規劃，降低難度和提高學習意願，協助雅思程度 4.5-7 分左右程度的考生學習，漸進式由單句演練到整篇作文的撰寫，擺脫教科書式的表達，以更道地的語句表達各類型的文句。

整合能力強化 ❷ 單句中譯英演練

在掌握文法句型後，學習者大多能拿到 7 分以上的寫作成績，英語句型多樣性是獲取高分的關鍵，現在請演練接下來的單句中譯英練習。請務必演練後再觀看答案，也可以搭配範文音檔強化對各句型的記憶。

❶ 當賈斯汀，《醜女貝蒂》裡的其中一位角色，拿到入學通知的拒絕信時，他告訴他的家人，他不想要等明年，以及他想要今年就要進他理想的學校就讀。

【參考答案】
When Justin, one of the characters in *Ugly Betty*, gets the rejection letter, he tells his family that he doesn't want next year, and he wants to go to his desired school this year.

❷ 他母親當時的男朋友，一位議員回應了他這個舉動，簡單且值得讚許。

【參考答案】
How his mother's boyfriend, a senator, responds to his reaction, is simple but commendable.

246

Unit 13 「成長型思維模式」和「固定型思維模式」對人們的學習和獲取成功影響甚距，請以具體實例解釋兩者間的差異。

❸ 他說這是需要時間的，而這也是為什麼要花費他數年，他才獲取現在的職位。

【參考答案】
He says it takes time, and this is why it takes him years to get his position now.

❹ 藉由分析他們對於挫折的反應，我們可以很清楚看到賈斯汀是位具有固定型思維模式的人，而議員卻具有成長型思維模式。

【參考答案】
By analyzing how they react to failures, we can clearly see that Justin is someone with a fixed mindset, whereas the senator possesses the growth mindset.

❺ 在《關鍵十年》，它也談論到成長型思維模式的重要性。「對於那些具有成長型思維模式者，失敗可能會讓人感到刺痛，但是他們將其視為是改進和改變的機會」。

【參考答案】
In *The Defining Decade*, it also talks about the importance of the growth mindset. "For those who have a growth mindset, failures

Part 3 雅思寫作 Task2 大作文

整合能力強化 ❹ 參考範文 ▶ MP3 010

經由先前的演練後，現在請看整篇範文並聆聽音檔

Given is a diagram **illustrating** the number of brown bears from 1949 to 2019. From 1949 **onward**, there has been a **consecutive fluctuation** due to the **severity** of the natural catastrophes. It is **intriguing** to note that after the same population went through **oscillation** at a ten-year interval, the number of brown bears remains the same to only a thousand in both 1949 and 2019.

提供的是一個圖表說明從 1949 到 2019 年棕熊的數量。從 1949 年推進，由於天災的嚴重程度，棕熊的數量一直受到波動。引人注目的是在族群經歷過每隔十年為期的擺動，棕熊數量在 1949 年和 2019 年間維持不變，僅僅 1000 隻。

From the onset, there was a slight climb to two thousand in 1959. Then the number **experienced exponential growth**, ballooning to 6,000 in 1969, a dramatic increase from 1959. Then a decade later, the number of brown bears **reached a plateau** and even to the **subsequent** ten years. In 1989, the sum of brown bears **pinnacled** at 9,000, but did not **remain constant** over the year. Instead, the number of brown bears **plummeted** to only 3,000 in 1999, a **dramatic decrease** from the previous decade. The number of brown bears failed to recover to the initial state, and encounter **a mild reduction** to 2,000 in 2009. Ultimately, the number of brown bears **descends** to only a thousand.

開始於 1959 年時有著些微的爬升來至 2000 隻。然後，數量經歷了指數成長，於 1969 年激增至 6000 隻，這是從 1959 年以來的急遽增加。10 年之後，棕熊的數量達到高原期，甚至持續到接下的 10 年。在 1989 年時，棕熊的總數來到巔峰的 9000 隻，但是並未於接下來的年間維持不變。取而代之的是，在 1999 年時，棕熊的數量重跌至僅剩 3000 隻，與前一個 10 年相比是個急遽的跌幅。棕熊數量未能回復至先前的水平，而在 2009 年經歷些微的減少至 2000 隻。最終，棕熊的數量降至僅剩 1000 隻。

In conclusion, the number of brown bears, after 70 years of **succession** due to natural **calamities**, only **endures a thousand**, the same as the number at the very beginning. (209 words)

總結，棕熊的數量，在經歷了 70 年天災的影響所造成的消長，僅僅只剩下 1000 隻，這個數量與最初相同。

有效點出眾多考生寫作分數卡在 6.5 分的原因
大幅強化應答實力

- ❶ 熟悉「圖表題常考字彙」跟其反義詞的用法、❷ 能靈活使用「圖表題常考字彙」其他詞性的用法並強化時態表達 ❸ 與「高階形容詞」做搭配 ❹ 把敘述**具體化** ❺ 學習高階圖表題動詞的使用 ❻ 搭配同位語表達 ❼ 搭配其他句型和 ❽ 比較差異處等等。

Instructions 使|用|說|明

 整合能力強化 ❹ 參考範文 ▶ *MP3 040*

經由先前的演練後，現在請看看整篇範文並聆聽音檔

When Justin, one of the characters in *Ugly Betty*, gets the rejection letter, he tells his family that he doesn't want next year, and he wants to go to his desired school this year. How his mother's boyfriend, a senator, responds to his reaction, is simple but commendable. He says it takes time, and this is why it takes him years to get his position now. By analyzing how they react to failures, we can clearly see that Justin is someone with a fixed mindset, whereas the senator possesses the growth mindset.

當賈斯汀，《醜女貝蒂》裡的其中一位角色，拿到入學通知的拒絕信時，他告訴他的家人，他不想要等明年，以及他想要今年就要進他理想的學校就讀。他母親當時的男朋友，一位議員回應了他這個舉動，簡單且值得讚許。他說這是需要時間的，而這也是為什麼要花費他數年，他才獲取現在的職位。藉由分析他們對於挫折的反應，我們可以很清楚看到賈斯汀是位具有固定思維模式的人，而議員卻具有成長型思維模式。

252

The two following bestsellers also discusses the concept of the growth mindset. In *The Defining Decade*, it also talks about the importance of the growth mindset. "For those who have a growth mindset, failures may sting but they are also viewed as opportunities for improvement and change." In *Mistakes I Made at Work*, Carol S. Dweck mentions "When you have a "growth mindset," you understand that mistakes and setbacks are an inevitable part of learning." Both clearly show the importance of thinking patterns and how it is going to affect the result.

下列兩位暢銷書作者也討論到了成長型思維模式的觀念。在《關鍵十年》，它也談論到成長型思維模式的重要性。「對於那些具有成長型思維模式者，失敗可能會讓人感到刺痛，但是他們將其視為是改進和改變的機會」。在《我在工作中所犯的錯誤》，卡洛斯·德維克提及「當你具有成長型思維模式時，你了解到錯誤和挫折是學習中不可或缺的一部分」。兩者清楚地顯示出思考模式的重要性，以及這會如何影響到結果。

People possessing a fixed mindset, someone like Justin, cannot seem to handle rejections well, and this more or

253

範文均錄音，內建「西方寫作邏輯腦」，省時且下筆快如神
暢銷書加持，寫出與眾不同文章、驚艷考官

- 獨家規劃寫作也搭配錄音，Task 1 圖表題寫作和 Task 2 大作文均附錄音，滿足更多「聽力」學習型的學習者，用零碎的時間就能準備好雅思寫作雙題型。
- 完全省掉拿數本文法書和英文寫作書不斷苦讀，文法選擇題都答對但仍寫不出好句子的困擾。
- 大作文有數本暢銷書籍神加持，不補習、不求人寫作也能立即速成。
  - *Mistakes I Made at Work*《我在工作中所犯的錯誤》
  - *The Defining Decade*《關鍵十年》
  - *The Job* 《工作》
  - *Rich Dad Poor Dad*《窮爸爸富爸爸》
  - *What I Wish I Knew When I was 20*《但願當我 20 歲時就知道的事》
  - *Originals*《創新》
  - *How Will You Measure Your Life*《你如何衡量你的人生》
  - *Where You Go Is Not Who You Will Be*《你所讀的學校並非你能成為什麼樣的人》
  - *The Promise of the Pencil :* how an ordinary person can create an extraordinary change" 《一支鉛筆的承諾：一位普通人如何能創造出驚人的改變》

Part 1 雅思寫作 Task1：精選高分字彙

CONTENTS

Part 2 雅思寫作 Task1：圖表題小作文

Part 3 雅思寫作 Task2：大作文

CONTENTS

常見倍數的用法、數量腰斬和暴跌的表達

★ 單元概述

　　這個單元介紹了**倍數**的用法，其實表達方式有非常多，考生較常使用 double 等。其實可以換成像是使用 twofold 等字或以數字形式加上 times 等，也可以多熟悉四倍以上的倍數單字，那些字因為較不常被考生使用，反而使用後文章在「用字得分」上面會有更好的效果。除了使用倍數來表達增幅，也可以使用強力動詞 **halve** 來表達獲利或數值的腰斬。此外，文章中還介紹了較特別的字 **nose-dive** 用來表示跌幅，halve 跟 nose-dive 若和倍數相關字搭配著用於表達增幅和跌幅的線條圖等，會使曲線圖作文生色不少喔！

圖表題高分字彙　▶ MP3 001

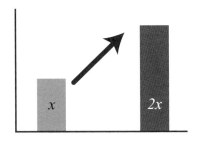

Twofold

【 **twofold** 兩倍的 】

■ Surprisingly, there was a **twofold** increase in the number of people playing the pinball in the night market in 2018.

令人感到吃驚的是在 2018 年，在夜市打彈珠的人數增加了兩倍。

【還能怎麼說】

■ Preference for whale meat has resulted in a **twofold** increase of recruitment for the fishermen in the area.

對鯨魚肉的偏好已經導致地區中招募捕魚人數的數量有了兩倍的成長。

■ According to the survey, the number of tourists visiting Germany increased **twofold** in 2017.

根據調查，拜訪德國的觀光人數在 2017 年時有了兩倍的成長。

☙ 小提點 ❧

Twofold 可以當作形容詞和副詞使用，有兩倍的和兩倍地的意思，而表達兩倍的用法還有 double, duplicate, two times 和 twice。其他倍數的表達還有數字+fold（eg. **fivefold**）or 數字+times（eg. three times），此外還有其他動詞的用法也可以記下並用於圖表題，像是 triple, **quadruple**, **quintuple**, **sextuple** 等等的。

21

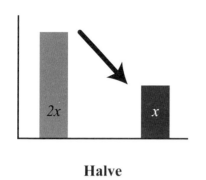

$2x$ x

Halve

【halve 將…對分，減半/腰斬】

■ As a country heavily reliant on the import of the ingredients, the higher price for raw materials has made the number of products nearly **halve** in the first quarter.

身為高度仰賴原料進口的國家，較高額的原物料價格已經導致產品的數量在第一季時腰斬了。

【還能怎麼說】

■ Due to the economic downturn, the payment for all executives in the company almost **halved** during the second quarter.

由於經濟蕭條，所有公司的高階主管的收入在第二季營運期間幾乎砍半。

■ Since profits from illegal hunting for marine creatures nearly **halved** in the last year, no one wants to invest more money in the company.

既然海洋生物非法盜獵的利潤在去年近乎砍半，沒有人想要在投資更多金錢再這間公司上。

❧ 小提點 ❧

Halve 的同義詞有 divide, dissect, split, share。這個字當動詞的用法可以適時運用在考試中增添表達力。例如前一句表達出數據是以倍數成長但後期數值卻是腰斬，比較不單調。

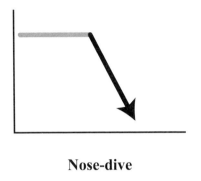

Nose-dive

【 nose-dive 價格等的暴跌 】

■ Best Airlines reported a 60% **nose-dive** in its third quarter profit to 25 million dollars.

倍斯特航空公司報告了它在第三季利潤暴跌了 60%來到兩千五百萬元。

【還能怎麼說】

■ Badly injured by the bidding war, the stock price of the Best Airlines took a **nose-dive**, making the total revenue dip to 4 million dollars.

因為競價戰而受到嚴重傷害，倍斯特航空公司的股價暴跌，使得整體營收降至四百萬元。

■ Because of an 80% **nose-dive** in the fourth quarter, Best Airlines is unable to win the support from the shareholders.

因為在第四季有著 80%的暴跌，倍斯特航空公司無法得到股東們的支持。

&ec; 小提點 &ec;

Nose-dive 這個字蠻特別的，也鮮少考生使用，非常建議考生使用，它用於表達「**數值的暴跌**」，也比單純僅使用 a dramatic decrease 好且高階，可以多練習這個字和 **after or before** 一起搭配的句型，在一個數值暴跌之前或之後...，圖形變化為何呢？

23

表達數值的三個超好搭高分字：指數成長、些微增加和驚人式增加

★ 單元概述

　　這個單元介紹了在雅思寫作的圖表題中獲取高分的考生都會使用到這幾個字。除了增加和倍數等用字外，使用 **exponential** 來表示數值是呈現指數增長的會蠻特別的，另一個相關的高階字 lackluster 也可以使用喔！都是搭配 growth。還有另外兩個字是 **staggering** 和 **negligible** 也常用於表達數值變化的形容，但都是蠻高階的字，除了形容名詞 increase or decrease 等字外，建議加上數值或幅度在中間，讓表達更具體，太模糊的表達像是 a decrease in 1990 不建議使用，可以修正成 **a staggering 50% decrease** in 1990 讓表達更完整喔！

圖表題高分字彙 ▶ *MP3 002*

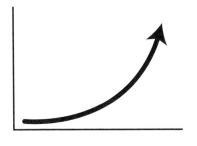

Exponential

【**exponential** 呈指數型增長的】

- Despite a lack of consumer confidence, the latest product experienced **exponential** growth in the past few weeks.
  儘管缺乏消費者信心，最新推出的產品在過去幾周感受到指數性的成長。

【還能怎麼說】

- Despite lackluster growth in the cosmetics segment, **exponential** growth of five other major products has made the company dominant in the industry.
  儘管在化妝品部分無亮眼的成長，在其他五項主要產品的指數性成長已經使得公司主導整個產業。

- **Exponential** growth of the smartphone has swayed the viewpoints in a shareholder meeting.
  智慧型手機的指數性成長已經使得股東會議中的觀點有所動搖。

∾ 小提點 ∾

Exponential 這個字非常重要，是一個蠻高階的字但又能表達出圖形呈現上升的趨勢，也可以替代掉很多字的用法，更簡潔地呈現出數值的變化，小作文出現線條圖等時，請務必用這個字。

Negligible

【 negligible 可忽略的、微不足道的 】

- A **negligible** 5% profit in this month cannot even cover the operating costs of the company for a week.

  在這個月的微幅 5%利潤甚至無法支付公司這周的營運成本。

【 還能怎麼說 】

- Since household appliances only bring in a **negligible** 2% profit, the head of the company has decided to cut the division in half.

  既然家電用品僅帶來微幅的 2%利潤，公司負責人已經決定要把部門砍半。

- The profit seems **negligible** to the eyes of the CMO, since his paycheck is greater than that.

  在首席營銷官的眼中利潤幾乎微乎其為，因為他的收入還高於該預算。

☙ 小提點 ☙

這個字也是高分用字，請務必要使用，包含了像是 a negligible 2% increase 等等，別單純只使用 there was an increase in 1999，用上這個字加上數字或數值，更具體表達和描述圖形變化，這樣才會拿到 7 以上的分數喔！

Part 1
雅思寫作 Task1⋯精選高分字彙

Part 2
雅思寫作 Task1⋯圖表題小作文

Part 3
雅思寫作 Task2⋯大作文

Staggering

【 **staggering** 驚人的】

■ There was a **staggering** 150% decrease in the price of apples because of the overproduction.
因為過量的生產，蘋果的價格有著驚人的 150%跌幅。

【還能怎麼說】

■ Due to a lack of rain this season, it is highly likely that the price of fruits is going to be **staggering**.
由於這季缺雨，水果的價格極可能會很驚人。

■ A **staggering** 50% rise in price of fruits and vegetables after the typhoon is expected.
在颱風過境後，蔬果的價格有著驚人的 50%漲幅是可預知的。

❧ 小提點 ❧

這個字也很重要，可以使用 a staggering 2% increase 等表達讓描述更具體，這個字和 negligible 有異曲同工之妙，這兩個字在雅思寫作高分的考生中很常見喔，快使用吧！

上漲、下跌和進入
回復期的三個高分表達

★ 單元概述

　　這個單元介紹了三個能讓圖表題增色但考生卻較少使用的字。考生太常使用 decrease, increase or decline 等字，而在表達數值「猛增」或「暴漲」時可以運用 **soar** 這個動詞，數值暴跌時使用 **plummet**。使用這兩個動詞會獲得更高的評價，某部分原因是「字詞使用」，能越簡潔地描述會被視為是「較佳的表達」，像是使用 a dramatic increase，不如單純的使用 soar 就夠了，此外 soar 還能再用副詞修飾，用高階副詞搭配又能更高分，完勝 a dramatic increase。最後是 **recovery**，可以用於表達數值上升或下降後來到一個回復期，也是很不錯的字喔！

Part 1
雅思寫作 Task1：精選高分字彙

Part 2
雅思寫作 Task1：圖表題小作文

Part 3
雅思寫作 Task2：大作文

圖表題高分字彙　▶ MP3 003

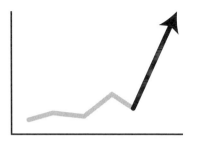

Soar

【**soar** 猛增、暴漲、高漲】

■ The value of the castle **soared** 55.8% in the first week of September, but has had a steady decline in the following weeks.
城堡的價值在 9 月第一周後暴漲 55.8%，但是在接續幾周有著持續性的跌幅。

【還能怎麼說】

■ Best Airlines saw its revenue **soar** 150%, from 60 million dollars to 90 million dollars.
倍斯特航空公司目睹其營收暴漲了 150%，從原先的 6 千萬元來到 9 千萬元。

■ At the end of the August, the price of the strawberry **soared** to a new all-time high, 1000 dollars per kilo, which made farmers worrisome.
在八月底，草莓的價格暴漲到新高點，來到每公斤 1000 元，此舉讓農夫感到擔憂。

⚘ 小提點 ⚘

Soar 當動詞其實也較少考生使用，建議可以多用，考生太常用 increase 了，可以在語句切換時用上 soar or balloon，能讓你的作文生色不少呢！重點是你會更高分 XD。

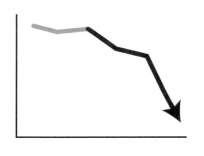

Plummet

【 plummet 暴跌、重挫 】

- The stock of the Best Airlines **plummeted** on Thursday trading due to the air crash accident earlier this week.

  倍斯特航空公司的股票，在周四股市交易時由於稍早的墜機意外事件而重挫。

【 還能怎麼說 】

- After the rumour of the sexual abuse incident, the reputation of the product **plummeted** to number 98 in the survey conducted by Yahoo.

  在性虐待謠傳事件後，由奇摩所進行的調查中顯示，產品的名聲重挫至第 98 名。

- After maintaining a five-week high, the stock price **plummeted** to the lowest level because leakage of the deterioration of the CEO's health condition.

  在維持連續五周的新高後，股價重挫至新低點，因為 CEO 健康情況惡化的消息的走漏。

∽ 小提點 ∽

Plummet 表達數值急遽下跌，與其使用 a dramatic decrease 不如直接使用 plummet 一個動詞，表達更高階，而且使用的字更少。

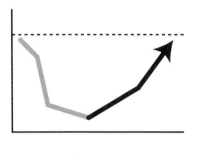

Recovery

【recovery 重獲、恢復】

■ After a steep decline to the lowest point in history, the Dow Jones Industrial Average experienced a **recovery**, obtaining 1000 points later this week.

在陡直的下降後來到歷史新低點，道瓊工業指數經歷的回復期，在這周稍後回復至 1000 點。

【還能怎麼說】

■ From the expert's perspective, the stock market actually needs more than a three-month **recovery** to the previous level.

從專家的觀點來看，股市實際上需要多於三個月的回復期才能回到先前的水準。

■ To everyone's relief, the stock market had a bounce-back earlier this week, but the **recovery** might be longer than predicted.

令每個人都感到如釋重負的是，股市在這周稍早有了回彈，但是回復期可能比預測來的長。

❧ 小提點 ❧

Recovery 是較不容易表達但可以運用很廣的字，它表達出數據變化在某個低點後，數值開始上升至回復期，較少考生用到這個字，通常僅很 general 的表達出 there was a slight/steady increase，可以在這樣的語句表達後用上 recovery 等字，這樣更完整。

31

表達下降、顯著差異和進入高原期的常見表達

★ 單元概述

　　Decrease 前面有提過，decrease 和 increase 真的太常使用了，不過還是要熟悉它當**動詞**和**名詞**的用法並正確使用出，它很好搭配，可以記它的**高階**同、反義字並搭配高階形容詞使用，效果也很好喔。另一個高分表達是 **in stark contrast**，在雅思寫作獲取高分的考生也常用這個字，建議多練習這個片語的造句，讓你離高分更近。最後一個字是 **plateau**，這個字蠻不錯的，但是也較少考生用到，蠻可惜的，在數值的上升或下降後，其實有時候會來到**高原期**，這時候可以運用這個高階字，讓文章更加分喔！

Part 1
雅思寫作 Task1：精選高分字彙

Part 2
雅思寫作 Task1：圖表題小作文

Part 3
雅思寫作 Task2：大作文

圖表題高分字彙　▶ MP3 004

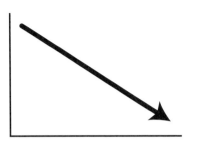

Decrease

【**decrease** 減少、降低】

■ The export of the watermelon rose to 1000 tons in September 2018, while there was an immense **decrease** in other fruits.
在 2018 年，西瓜的出口量上漲至一千噸，而在其他水果方面則有巨大的跌幅。

【還能怎麼說】

■ Opposition for the import of watermelons has led to a **decrease** in the purchase, since most consumers now favour exotic goods.
反對進口西瓜導致購買力的下滑，因為大多數的消費者偏好外國的商品。

■ The price of watermelons **decreased** by 5% in the early June, but maintained pretty stable throughout July.
西瓜價格在六月初跌了 5%，但是在整個七月期間則維持相當穩定的價格。

⤳ 小提點 ⤳

Decrease 的同義字有 decline, fall, drop，不得不說這四個字非常常見，可以都記起來並注意這四個字的三態變化，使用 drop 的過去式要用 dropped，decrease 的同義字有 **diminish**, **divide**, **subtract**, **reduce** 等，而反義字有 **increase**, **augment**, **multiply** 等等。

33

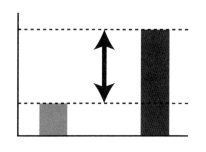

Stark

【stark 明顯地、突出地】

- In **stark** contrast, bones excavating at the archaeological site showed a strong correlation with remains in the Pacific Ocean.

  與之形成鮮明對比的是，在考古遺址上挖掘出的骨頭顯示出與太平洋的遺骸有著高強度的關聯性。

【還能怎麼說】

- In **stark** contrast to last year's animation, which put much emphasis on simulation of real-life animals, this year visual effects and sound effects will be the key.

  與去年的動畫有著顯著差異的是，去年將重點放在模擬現實生活中的動物，而今年的視覺效果和聲光效果則是關鍵。

- In **stark** contrast, tech stocks had a significant drop of around 52% due to a lack of consumer confidence.

  與之形成鮮明對比的是，科技股有著近 52%的顯著跌幅，因為消費者缺乏信心。

❧ 小提點 ❧

Stark 這個字最常用的用法是 in stark contrast，常見在圖表題總結處，代表顯著差異處，可以多造幾句各類型圖表和趨勢的句子並使用這個片語，讓表達更高分喔！

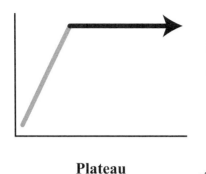

Plateau

【plateau 高原；（上升後的）穩定水準（或時期）】

- After the succession, the population of the polar bears had a steady climb, reaching a **plateau** in the following year.

在消長過後，北極熊的族群數有著穩定的攀升，在接下來的年度中達到高原期。

【還能怎麼說】

- Eradication of invasive species was the main reason why Australia animals became less vulnerable and the number staying at a **plateau** since.

摧毀外來種是澳洲動物較不易受攻擊的主因，此後數量將維持在穩定的水準。

- Due to unknown reasons, tech stocks, after reaching a **plateau** in the Wednesday trading, began to drop significantly.

由於不明的原因，科技股在周三的股市交易達到高原期後，開始顯著地下降。

❧ 小提點 ❧

Plateau 這個字較少被考生使用，但它用來描述例如族群數量等達到一個平衡穩定的狀態，圖表題中常會有的趨勢，在上漲或下跌後漸漸呈現出一個**平衡穩定**的狀態，就可以使用這個字。

表達數值達到巔峰、降至最低點和產生波動

★ 單元概述

　　Peak 是考生很常用的字，但是要高分的話其實除了正確使用 peak 當名詞和動詞時的用法外，很重要的一點是用 peak 更高階的同義字來表達，讓考官知道你跟其他考生的差異處，你用上更高階的字彙。與 peak 相反的是最低點 at the lowest point，但是建議用其他字像是單元中介紹的 **bottom out**，這個字在英文報章雜字中也常出現，也是高分的字彙，建議多練習這個字的各種表達。最後介紹的是 fluctuation，數值除了急遽的升降外，也會有波動的情況，這時候可以使用 fluctuation 這個較高階的字，考生也可以多練習它的動詞 fluctuate 的用法喔！

圖表題高分字彙　▶ MP3 005

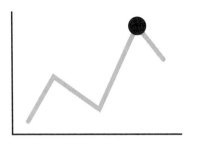

Peak

【**Peak** 頂端、最高點】

- Thanks largely to the help of the retailers, smartphones have sold more than 5 million units in its debut, reaching a **peak** in the second week.

大部分是幸虧零售商們的幫助，智慧型手機在首次亮相時，已經銷售超過五百萬支，在第二周時達到高峰。

【還能怎麼說】

- Despite a slight decline of 6.9% in shipment in July, the smartphone sales eventually made a comeback, reaching its **peak** at 10 million units in August.

儘管在七月的運輸上有些微的 6.9%跌幅，智慧型手機的銷售起死回生，在八月時達到一千萬支。

- After launching its flagship products, home appliances of Best Company had unprecedented growth in history, **peaking** at 6 million units in 2018.

在推出旗艦產品後，倍斯特公司的家電用品有著史無前例的成長，在 2018 年時達到六百萬支。

≫ 小提點 ≪

考生常使用 at the highest point，不過沒有比單純使用 peak 簡潔。另外就是，peak 的同義字有 **top, summit, pinnacle, apex** 等。

37

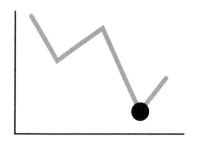

Bottom out

【 bottom out 降至最低點 】

- Sales of smartphones have **bottomed out**, but the launch of the flagship one has turned things around.
  手機銷售已經降至最低點，但是旗艦機的推出讓銷售扭轉乾坤。

【 還能怎麼說 】

- After a few bounces, tech stocks failed to stay at a certain point and eventually **bottomed out**, shocking all foreign investors.
  在幾次回彈後，科技股未能維持在特定點，而股價最終降至最低點，讓所有外國投資客都感到震驚。

- Sexual discrimination lawsuits have made viewership of Best TV **bottom out**, exasperating multiple executives.
  性歧視的訴訟讓倍斯特電視的收視率降至最低點，此舉惹怒的許多高階主管。

☙ 小提點 ❧

在表達最高點或最低點時，常見考生會使用 at the lowest point or at the highest point，在表達達到最低點時可以改用 **bottom out**，其實在新聞等也常使用這個用法，也會比單純使用 at the lowest point 表達更好喔！

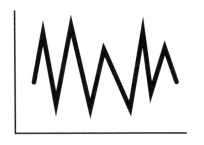

Fluctuation

【 fluctuation 波動 】

- Increase in tariffs was the main reason why the price had such a **fluctuation** in the past few weeks.
- 關稅的增加是價格在過去幾周有如此波動的主因。

【 還能怎麼說 】

- Price **fluctuations** in domestic products have made housewives groaned and indignant.
  家用產品的價格波動已經讓許多家庭主婦們怨聲載道和感到憤怒。
- Before reaching a plateau, the price of rice had several **fluctuations** due to a lack of supply and visiting of hurricanes.
  由於缺乏供給和颶風到訪的原因,在米價達到高原期之前,有幾次波動 。

❧ 小提點 ❧

在描述數值的起伏時,與其用 rise and fall or ups and downs,直接使用 fluctuate 會更加分喔,建議同時熟悉 **fluctuate** 和 **fluctuation** 的用法,在描述數值起伏時能更佳。

三個高頻使用
的副詞和形容詞

★ 單元概述

　　這個單元介紹了三個常見的詞 steadily, gradually, significantly，它們的形容詞也常在圖表題的使用中出現，所以同步熟悉**形容詞**和**副詞**的運用和搭配對於提升圖表題的分數來說是很關鍵的。這三個字在程度的表達上也非常不同，很適合拿來練習，形容詞的話可以多記下後面常搭配的名詞，而副詞的話可以看下句中使用的動詞，最後根據圖中的數據變化程度運用在其中，如果是大幅度的增加則用 **significant**，而如果是逐漸增加則使用 **gradual**，能靈活運用這三個字的兩種詞性就向獲取高分邁進一大步了。

🍎 **圖表題高分字彙** ▶ *MP3 006*

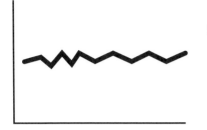

Steadily/ Steady

【 **Steadily/steady 穩定地/的** 】

■ After the slowdown in car sales, Best Automobile Company has differentiated itself from other car companies and the sales figure has remained **steady** since then.

在汽車銷售呈現衰退後，倍斯特汽車公司已經與其他汽車公司作出區隔化，從那之後銷售數字就維持穩定。

【 **還能怎麼說** 】

■ Tickets of Best Airlines have sold **steadily** over the year, making shareholders convince that it's worth investing.
倍斯特航空公司在這年已經有穩定的銷售，讓股東們深信其是值得投資的。

■ After the initial fluctuation in prices, tech stocks have managed to maintain a **steady** climb, alleviating the doubts among investors.
在最初幾次的價格波動後，科技股已經設法維持穩定的爬升，減緩投資者之間的質疑。

❧ 小提點 ❧

Steady 後常搭配名詞（例如：decline, climb, jump...）等可以表達出很多樣的狀態，它的同義字還有 constant, fixed, inert, regular, incessant, ceaseless 等等，而反義詞有 **unsteady, changeable** 等等。

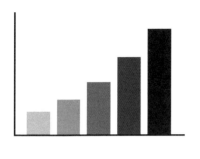

Gradually/ Gradual

【 gradually/gradual 逐漸地/的 】

- There has been a **gradual** decrease in the number of giraffes given birth in the zoo since 2018.

  自從 2018 年後，動物園中長頸鹿的出生數量遞減。

【 還能怎麼說 】

- Unable to meet the need of consumers, fashion clothes are **gradually** being replaced by inexpensive, affordable, simple dresses.

  無法達到消費者的需求，流行服飾逐漸被不昂貴、可負擔得起和簡單的女裝所取代。

- Despite a **gradual** increase of 2.5% in the Tuesday trading, transportation stocks plunged almost 75% on Friday morning.

  儘管在周二的股市交易上有漸進的 2.5%成長，運輸股在周五早晨大幅重挫近 75%。

❧ 小提點 ❧

考生可以多熟悉像是 gradually or gradual 的用法，適時的切換在語句表達中，而表達數據是微幅成長的用法還有使用 moderate 等字，例如 moderate increase/decrease，可以把它記下來。

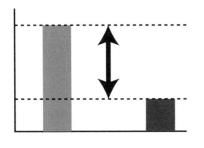

Significantly/ Significant

【 significantly/significant 顯著地/的 】

■ Best bookstores have **significantly** lessened the lengthy procedures, so consumers are able to get their purchase within a day.
倍斯特書店已經大幅地減輕了冗長的程序，所以消費者能夠在一天之內拿到他們的購物品項。

【 還能怎麼說 】

■ Tickets of Best Airlines have dropped **significantly** due to the safety concern on the Friday hijacking incident.
倍斯特航空公司的購票率由於周五的劫機事件所產生的安全疑慮而明顯下滑。

■ The profit of the Best Airlines has risen remarkably to 8 billion dollars, a **significant** 200% increase from last year.
倍斯特航空公司已經有著顯著的漲幅來到 80 億元，比起去年有著驚人的 200% 增幅。

❦ 小提點 ❦

不得不說 significantly 在圖表題中很常用到，除了用這個字表達改變的幅度很大外，也可以使用像是 **remarkable, noteworthy, notable** 等等，除了副詞和形容詞用法外，也可以使用像是 also noteworthy is the fact that⋯等句型來呈現圖表的狀態。

43

減少的名詞用法、上升的各時態表達和激增的表達

★ 單元概述

　　前面有提過 decrease 等字很常使用，reduce 等字也是，但是如果可以改用名詞 reduction 當主詞反而是更加分的，考生可以熟悉**名詞當主詞**的用法，取代使用動詞的表達。另一個字彙是 **rise** 表示增幅，能運用的範圍真的很廣，但要注意時態就是了，還有 rise 當名詞和動詞時的用法，這些都是得分關鍵。最後介紹的是 **balloon** 考生較少使用到這樣的字彙，balloon 當動詞的用法運用在圖表題是很加分的，建議多練習這個字在各類主題中數值激增時的造句練習！

圖表題高分字彙 ▶ *MP3 007*

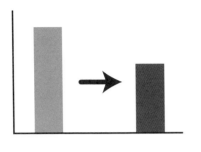

Reduction

【**Reduction** 減少、降低】

■ The profit of Best Airlines has significantly slashed due to a **reduction** in passengers.
由於搭機乘客數的降低，倍斯特航空公司的利潤大幅削減了。

【還能怎麼說】

■ A **reduction** in signing up for the course has reflected the shifting in trend among school students.
修該課的人數降低反映出學校學生對趨勢的轉變。

■ A **reduction** in the consumption of snakes is a good thing for the animal conservation.
攝食蛇的人數降低對於動物保育來説是件好事。

❧ 小提點 ❧

在表達減少或降低時常見的用法有使用動詞像 reduce 等字，其實改成使用名詞在句型表達上比使用動詞較難造句，當然也比較高分，可以多練習使用名詞 **reduction** 或類似的名詞進行造句，造句當然越細節性描述該圖表狀態越好喔！

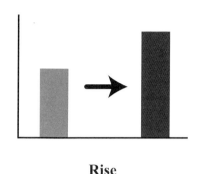

Rise

【rise 上升、上漲】

■ The population of crabs **rose** by 250% in 2017-2018, making the price of the crab significantly lower than that in 2016.

在 2017 年至 2018 年螃蟹的族群數量有著 250%的上漲，使得螃蟹的價格比起 2016 年時更為低廉。

【還能怎麼說】

■ Despite the fact that there was a **rise** earlier this month, corn farmers claimed that the production was still below the optimal level.

儘管在這個月稍早有著上漲，玉米農宣稱生產量仍低於適宜的等級。

■ The prices for most beverages have **risen** by 9% to 12%, a significant burden for consumers nowadays.

大多數飲料的價格從 9%上漲到 12%，對於消費者來說是個很大的負擔。

❧ 小提點 ❧

Rise 看似簡單，但是在圖表題中常被考生誤用，誤用常見的是在時態的部分，**rise 的三態是 rise, rose, risen**。Rise 在表達上升或上漲時，同義字還有 advance, ascend, go up, increase 等等，考生可以在其他語句中做替換。

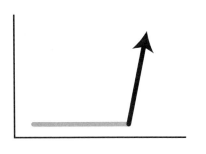

Balloon

【 balloon 激增 】

- Tuition loans **ballooned** to 19.8 million dollars at the end of the March 2019, up from 65% from 12 million dollars in 2016.
- 學貸已從 2019 年三月底激增至 1980 萬元，從 2016 年的 1200 萬元上升了 65%。

【 還能怎麼說 】

- Fruit prices dipped by 25% in July 2019, whereas vegetable prices **ballooned** to 80% higher.
  2019 年 7 月水果的價格降了 25%，而蔬菜的價格卻激增了超過 80%。
- Manipulation of the procedures has made the sales **balloon** to a new all-time high.
  程序的操控已經讓銷售激增至新高點。

☙ 小提點 ☙

大家都知道 balloon 是氣球，但較少人知道它動詞的用法表示**激增**，或許我們都背過很多字，但是該字另一詞性的用法或較少為人所知的用法就是考點或加分點，在圖表題中可以表達類似這樣的字，讓作文更突出，而不是 increase or decrease 用到底，balloon 的同義字還有 **increase, enlarge, multiply, augment, magnify, amplify, heighten** 等等，建議都背起來。

47

維持不變、成反比和下降趨勢的表達

★ 單元概述

    Remain constant 是考生必會的用法了，在圖表題中很常需要表達出數值維持於一個**恆定值**，也要特別注意在時態的使用。另一個是成反比，可以在圖表題作文中穿插使用這類的表達，不會很呆版的僅使用增加或減少來表達數值的變化，另外也可以熟悉成正比的用法。最後介紹的是 downward 跟成正比或成反比有異曲同工之妙，考生還蠻常使用上的，最常見的表達是 an overall downward trend，downward or upward 用於表示趨勢的變化，和其他各主題的動詞、名詞、形容詞和副詞表達的增加或減少穿插搭配使用，可以迅速豐富表達，讓考官驚艷喔！

圖表題高分字彙 ▶ *MP3 008*

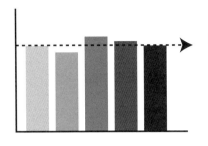

Remain constant

Part 1
雅思寫作 Task1：精選高分字彙

Part 2
雅思寫作 Task1：圖表題小作文

Part 3
雅思寫作 Task2：大作文

【Remain constant 維持穩定】

■ Despite the rivalry among numerous Airlines whether it is domestic or international, profits of Best Airlines have **remained constant** these years.

儘管面對著許多航空公司的競爭，不論是國內線或是國際線，倍斯特航空公司的利潤在這幾年都維持穩定。

- -

【還能怎麼說】

■ The monthly fee of the smartphone charged by Best Cellphone will **remain constant** in the following years.
倍斯特手機索取的智慧型手機月費在接續幾年會維持不變。

■ Despite its total revenue being shrunk in the first quarter, the profits in the subsequent quarters **remained constant**.
儘管整體的營收在第一季有萎縮，在接續幾季利潤將維持穩定。

- -

❧ 小提點 ❧

在直線圖、線條圖等圖形中，要表達數據達到一個恆定或維持在一個狀態時，常見的表達可使用 **remain constant**，除此之外也可以使用穩定的或穩定地的相關詞彙（例如：stable or steady 等）來表達狀態或程度。更進階的方式有使用 **stability**，即將形容詞或副詞**名詞化**當主詞，這樣語句會更高分喔！

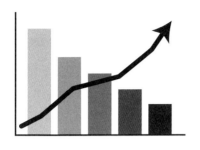

Inversely proportional

【 inversely proportional 成反比 】

- The rate of the basic metabolism is **inversely proportional** to the body weight.
  基礎代謝率跟身體體重成反比。

【 還能怎麼說 】

- The number of the subscription is actually **inversely proportional** to that of the audience watching the show.
  訂閱的數量實際上跟觀看節目的觀眾數量成反比。
- The harmful substance in marine creatures is not **inversely proportional** to the weight.
  海洋生物中的有害物質跟體重並不是成反比。

෧ 小提點 ෧

除了使用形容詞和副詞等表達語句外，建議適時的使用像是成反比和成正比的相關詞彙去呈現圖像的趨勢讓表達更不呆板，除了成反比外，成正比的英文是 **be (directly) proportional to/ in (direct) to**，可以平常就練習到在寫圖表題作文時至少使用到此表達一次。

【 downward 向下、日趨沒落的 】

■ There was an overall **downward** trend in the consumption of pearl milk tea in 2018.

在 2018 年珍珠奶茶的消費呈現出整體下降的趨勢。

Downward

【還能怎麼說】

■ Despite an overall **downward** trend in subscription, Best Newspaper has advertising revenues to balance the deficit.

儘管在訂閱方面有著整體下降的趨勢，倍斯特報紙利用廣告營收來平衡赤字。

■ Before experiencing a significant climb in the Thursday trading, there was an overall **downward** trend in green energy stocks.

在週四的股市交易中經歷顯著的爬升後，綠能股有著整體下滑的趨勢。

❧ 小提點 ❧

除了成正比和成反比可以用於表達趨勢的變化外，可以使用例句中的字彙 downward，最常見的就是 an overall downward trend，downward 的同義字還有 descending, going down, sliding, slipping，建議可以使用 descending，像在字詞使用上，**descending** 就比用 going down 高一階，而**反義字是 upward**，可以多練習這個字的例句。

UNIT 01

雙地圖題：
遊樂場場區位置變化圖

You should spend about 20 minutes on this task

The diagram below shows an amusement park that opened in 2018 and it contained six main facilities. To counter with growing tourists, the owner has discussed with several engineers about the renovation of the amusement park in 2035. Discuss several changes about these two.

Summarize the information by selecting and reporting the main features, and make comparisons where relevant.

Write at least 150 words

整合能力強化 ❶ 實際演練

請搭配左頁的題目和下方的圖片進行圖表題寫作的演練。

Amusement Park 2018

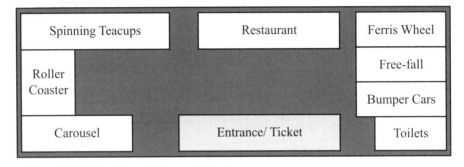

Amusement Park 2035

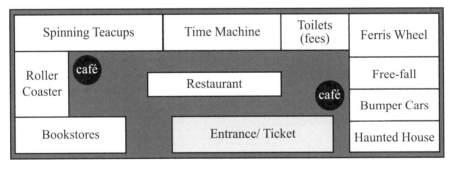

整合能力強化 ❷ 單句中譯英演練

在掌握文法句型後,學習者大多能拿到 7 分以上的寫作成績,英語句型多樣性是獲取高分的關鍵,現在請演練接下來的單句中譯英練習。請務必演練後再觀看答案,也可以搭配範文音檔強化對各句型的記憶。

❶ 遊樂園原創於 2018 年,是個長方形區塊包含著六個主要設施提供選擇。它包含了典型的設施,一般的遊樂園都有:旋轉咖啡杯、雲霄飛車、旋轉木馬、摩天輪、自由落體和碰碰車。

_____

_____

【參考答案】

Amusement Park was originated in 2018, a rectangular area that had six features to choose from. It consisted of typical features that normal amusement park has: spinning teacups, roller coaster, carousel, Ferris wheel, free-fall, and bumper cars.

❷ 引人注目的是廁所的地點已經從接近入口處移至時光機和摩天輪中間,而且是要收費的,這是史無前例的。

_____

_____

【參考答案】

It is intriguing to note that the location of the toilets has moved from near the entrance to between Time Machine and Ferris Wheel, and are charged with fees, unprecedented.

❸ 從所提供的資訊，位於入口處左側的旋轉木馬在 2035 年時會被書
店所取代。

_____

_____

【參考答案】

From the information provided, carousel situated at the left of the
entrance will be replaced by bookstores in 2035.

❹ 另一項會新增的設施是時光機，而愛好者可以體驗回到過去特定
時間點的特效。

_____

_____

【參考答案】

Another feature that will be joined is Time Machine, and fans can
experience special effects of going back to a specific timeframe.

❺ 兩個咖啡廳也會新增以迎合日益增加的參觀者，而餐廳將會移至
遊樂園的中間處。

_____

_____

【參考答案】

Two cafes will be added to encounter a growing number of
visitors, whereas restaurants will be moving to the middle of the
amusement park.

整合能力強化 ❸ 段落拓展

TOPIC

The diagram below shows an amusement park that opened in 2018 and it contained six main facilities. To counter with growing tourists, the owner has discussed with several engineers about the renovation of the amusement park in 2035. Discuss several changes about these two.

Summarize the information by selecting and reporting the main features, and make comparisons where relevant.

Step 1　　這題的話要注意有兩個地圖並注意時間點，因為這影響到時態的使用，重點也是放在比較這兩個圖形的異同。通常時間點是在兩個過去的時間點，這題的第二個地圖是在 2035 年，所以要使用表示未來的時態。有了這些概念並知道要注意時態表達後就可以開始描述了。

Step 2　　兩個地圖中沒有變動的部分和新增的設施都是描述點。先描述第一個地圖和主要的遊樂設施。

Step 3　接著描述接下來遊樂園會經歷的改變，有五個主要設施和入口處是維持不變的部分，再來描述新增的部分，廁所的移動和將會收費（這是史無前例的），還有時光機和鬼屋的新增，書店會取代旋轉木馬，和時光機特色的描述，咖啡廳的增加以應對日增的遊客。

Step 4　最後總結出，遊樂園會經歷的改變和簡略描述改變處，最後結尾描述一項特色，例如咖啡廳的增加能夠提升體驗。

經由先前的演練後，現在請看整篇範文並聆聽音檔

Amusement Park was originated in 2018, **a rectangular area that** had six features to choose from. It consisted of typical features that normal amusement park has: spinning teacups, roller coaster, carousel, Ferris wheel, free-fall, and bumper cars.

遊樂園原創於 2018 年，是個長方形區塊包含著六個主要設施提供選擇。它包含了典型的設施，一般的遊樂園都有：旋轉咖啡杯、雲霄飛車、旋轉木馬、摩天輪、自由落體和碰碰車。

According to the source, Amusement Park **will be undergoing** a series of changes to meet with picky fans. In 2035, five main features and the entrance will remain in the same location. It is **intriguing** to note that the location of the toilets has moved from near the entrance to between Time Machine and Ferris Wheel, and are charged with fees, unprecedented. From the information provided, carousel situated at the left of the entrance **will be replaced by** bookstores in 2035. Another feature that will be joined is Time Machine, and fans can experience special effects of going back to a specific timeframe. Two cafes will be added to encounter a growing number of visitors, whereas restaurants will be moving to the middle of the amusement park. Also remarkable is the fact that haunted house will be included in 2035, where fans get to **experience terror and an adrenaline rush**.

根據消息來源，遊樂園將會經歷一系列的改變以迎合挑剔的愛好者。在 2035 年，五個主要的設施和入口處會維持在同樣的地點。引人注目的是廁所的地點已經從接近入口處移至時光機和摩天輪中間，而且是要收費的，這是史無前例的。從所提供的資訊，位於入口處左側的旋轉木馬在 2035 年時會被書店所取代。另一項會新增的設施是時光機，而愛好者可以體驗回到過去特定時間點的特效。兩個咖啡廳也會新增以迎合日益增加的參觀者，而餐廳將會移至遊樂園的中間處。值得注目的是在 2035 年會新增鬼屋，愛好者能夠體驗恐怖和腎上腺素分泌的激增。

Although Amusement Park will be having **moderate altercations**, it does contain the fundamental feature to every potential visitor. With addition of two cafes and so on, it will certainly elevate the experience.

儘管遊樂園將會有些微的改變，它仍包含對每個潛在拜訪者所需的基礎設施。隨著兩個咖啡廳的增加等，它確實能提升體驗。

UNIT
02
曲線圖題：
棕熊族群數量因為天災產生的波動

Writing Task 1

You should spend about 20 minutes on this task

The diagram below shows the number of the brown bears from 1949 to 2019. The population encountered several fluctuations due to natural disasters. The statistics conducted here measures the number of brown bears per decade.

Summarize the information by selecting and reporting the main features, and make comparisons where relevant.

Write at least 150 words

整合能力強化 ❶ 實際演練

請搭配左頁的題目和下方的圖片進行圖表題寫作的演練。

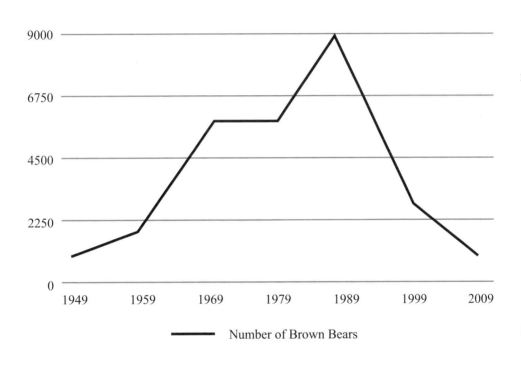

Natural Disasters
to the population of brown bears

——— Number of Brown Bears

在掌握文法句型後，學習者大多能拿到 7 分以上的寫作成績，英語句型多樣性是獲取高分的關鍵，現在請演練接下來的單句中譯英練習。請務必演練後再觀看答案，也可以搭配範文音檔強化對各句型的記憶。

❶ 從開始，於 1959 年有著些微的爬升來至 2000 隻。

_____

_____

【參考答案】

From the onset, there was a slight climb to two thousand in 1959.

❷ 然後，數量有了指數型的成長，於 1969 年時激增至 6000 隻，比起 1959 年有著急遽的增加。

_____

_____

【參考答案】

Then the number experienced exponential growth, ballooning to 6,000 in 1969, a dramatic increase from 1959.

❸ 而 10 年後，棕熊的數量達到高原期，而且持續到接下的 10 年。

_____

_____

【參考答案】

Then a decade later, the number of brown bears reached a plateau and even to the subsequent ten years.

❹ 在 1989 年，棕熊的總到達巔峰的 9000 隻，但是並未於接下來的年間維持不變。

_____

_____

【參考答案】

In 1989, the sum of brown bears pinnacled at 9,000, but did not remain constant over the year.

❺ 取而代之的是，在 1999 年棕熊數量重跌至僅剩 3000 隻，十年間驟降。

_____

_____

【參考答案】

Instead, the number of brown bears plummeted to only 3,000 in 1999, a dramatic decrease from the previous decade.

TOPIC

The diagram below shows the number of the brown bears from 1949 to 2019. The population encountered several fluctuations due to natural disasters. The statistics conducted here measures the number of brown bears per decade.

Summarize the information by selecting and reporting the main features, and make comparisons where relevant.

Step 1 先看題目的圖表題為何種形式，並統一以 **Given is/ are**...**diagram(s)**...or **A glance at the graph(s)**....等套句開頭，避免使用 the pic shows...等較低階的簡單句型。

- 在有年份的圖表題時，要避免每句開頭都是 in+年份，這樣會顯得單調，所以次句以 from 1949 **onward** 為開頭。

- 使用更能體現圖表題的專業字彙像是 **fluctuation**，並加上高階形容詞 consecutive，表示是一接續的波動，另外在天災的描述部分換個字彙，catastrophes。

- 下一句以 It is **intriguing** to note...為開頭，常見考生使用 it is interesting to note。若改用 intriguing 其實更好代表你知道這個較 interesting 高階的字彙。

■ 使用 went through **oscillation** 和 at a ten-year interval，代表族群經歷的擺動和圖表的年份是以 10 年為一個階段。接著描述族群的數量在最開頭和最尾端都是相同的數量，一千隻。

Step 2　接著也是避免使用 in+年份為開頭，改使用 from the onset 為開頭，並描述 there was a slight climb...。接續以高分慣用語 **exponential growth** 描述族群的成長，並搭配高階動詞 **balloon**（激增）表達出數量在 1969 年達到 6000 隻。

Step 3　接續改以 Then a decade later 開頭，外加高分語彙 **reached a plateau**，表達族群進入高原期，且此情況接續到下個十年。開頭使用 in 1989，搭配用高階字彙 **pinnacle** 表達族群達到顛峰，以 but 表達轉折接續搭配高階慣用語 did not **remain constant**，最後接續以高階字彙 plummet 描述族群的下降，此句後搭配使用「**同位語**」表達這與前年是 a dramatic decrease，最後使用名詞 a mild **reduction** 表達些微的下降，最後用動詞的表達 **descend** 結束描述的部分。

Step 4　最後總結，使用 **succession** 和 natural **calamities** 豐富表達，最後陳述出族群數量在開頭跟結尾維持一致。

經由先前的演練後，現在請看整篇範文並聆聽音檔

Given is a diagram illustrating the number of brown bears from 1949 to 2019. From 1949 **onward**, there has been a **consecutive** fluctuation due to the **severity** of the natural catastrophes. It is **intriguing** to note that after the same population went through oscillation at a ten-year interval, the number of brown bears remains the same to only a thousand in both 1949 and 2019.

提供的是一個圖表說明從 1949 年到 2019 年棕熊的數量。從 1949 年推進，由於天災的嚴重程度，棕熊的數量一直受到波動。引人注目的是在族群經歷過每隔十年為期的擺動，棕熊數量在 1949 年和 2019 年間維持不變，僅僅 1000 隻。

From the onset, there was a slight climb to two thousand in 1959. Then the number **experienced** exponential **growth**, ballooning to 6,000 in 1969, a dramatic increase from 1959. Then a decade later, the number of brown bears **reached a** plateau and even to the **subsequent** ten years. In 1989, the sum of brown bears pinnacled at 9,000, but did not remain constant over the year. Instead, the number of brown bears plummeted to only 3,000 in 1999, a **dramatic decrease** from the previous decade. The number of brown bears failed to recover to the initial state, and encounter **a mild reduction** to 2,000 in 2009. Ultimately, the number of brown bears **descends** to only a thousand.

開始於 1959 年時有著些微的爬升來至 2000 隻。然後，數量經歷了指數成長，於 1969 年激增至 6000 隻，這是從 1959 年以來的急遽增加。10 年之後，棕熊的數量達到高原期，甚至持續到接下的 10 年。在 1989 年時，棕熊的總數來到巔峰的 9000 隻，但是並未於接下來的年間維持不變。取而代之的是，在 1999 年時，棕熊的數量重跌至僅剩 3000 隻，與前一個 10 年相比是個急遽的跌幅。棕熊數量未能回復至先前的水平，而在 2009 年經歷些微的減少至 2000 隻。最終，棕熊的數量降至僅剩 1000 隻。

In conclusion, the number of brown bears, after 70 years of **succession** due to natural **calamities**, only **endures a thousand**, the same as the number at the very beginning. (209 words)

總結，棕熊的數量，在經歷了 70 年天災的影響所造成的消長，僅僅只剩下 1000 隻，這個數量與最初相同。

UNIT 03

雙生態金字塔圖題：
生物對應的層級和能量的流失

 Writing Task 1

You should spend about 20 minutes on this task

The diagram below includes two ecological pyramids, figure a and figure b. In figure a, you will find the representative of organisms in a specific layer. It is another realization of the concept of food chain or food web. In figure b, you will find that energy transferring from one to the next suffers energy loss, so there is only around 10% of the amount can be retained.

Summarize the information by selecting and reporting the main features, and make comparisons where relevant.

Write at least 150 words

整合能力強化 ❶ 實際演練

請搭配左頁的題目和下方的圖片進行圖表題寫作的演練。

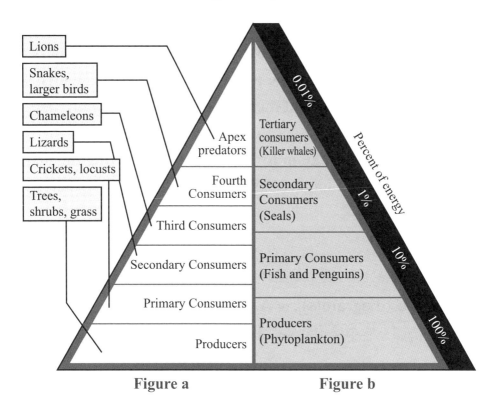

Ecological Pyramids

Figure a　　　　**Figure b**

TOPIC

The diagram below includes two ecological pyramids, figure a and figure b. In figure a, you will find the representative of organisms in a specific layer. It is another realization of the concept of food chain or food web. In figure b, you will find that energy transferring from one to the next suffers energy loss, so there is only around 10% of the amount can be retained.

Summarize the information by selecting and reporting the main features, and make comparisons where relevant.

Step 1　先看題目的圖表題為何種形式，並統一以 **Given is/ are**...**diagram(s)**...or **A glance at the graph(s)**....等套句開頭，避免使用 the pic shows...等較低階的簡單句句型。

Step 2　使用高階字 hierarchy，表達在 figure a 中區分成六個範疇，使用 ranging from A to B 的表達並於 A（producers）和 B（apex predators）後以形容詞子句補述（範文的底線部分），此舉可以增添句型 variety 的分數。

Step 3　接著使用 As can be seen from the graph 為開頭，接下來的描

70

述要注意兩個增添句型組成變化和增加字彙使用分數的地方。

■ 第一個是在表達「**組成**」的部分要熟悉 consist of 和 is made up of 等常見用法，避免一個句型用到底。在 producers 和 primary consumers 後面都用上不同的「**組成**」表達，並注意到 primary consumers 後省略了 **which are**。

■ 另一個注意的點是使用高階字彙增添風采，primary consumer 就是 **herbivore**（接續慣用語後），而 secondary consumer 就是 **omnivore**（使用同位語加上這個字），還有後面的肉食性動物 **carnivore**，這都能提升語彙表達。還在 third consumer 部分用上 **tertiary** 這個字。最後是避免直接使用金字塔的動物，換字改用 small insects 等取代。

Step 4　在 figure b 部分使用 **A glance at the graph(s)**....的套句開頭，接著 a more **simplified** version 表達跟 figure a 的差異處。接著使用 The **foundation** of..., the **subsequent** categories...和 The pinnacle of...，並以形容詞子句表達補述 whales。然後使用 It is **intriguing** to note..以及同位語 **a remarkable difference** from figure a.。然後可以參考範文中能量流失的描述，其實還有很多重點可以描述，例如比較頂端掠食者和生產者就可以描述僅能保留千分之一的能量。（考生可以多練習其它描述的句型）

Step 5　最後是總結這兩個圖表。

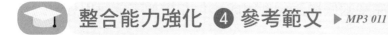
經由先前的演練後，現在請看整篇範文並聆聽音檔

Given are two figures (figure a and figure b) about ecological pyramids. The **hierarchy** in figure a divides into six categories, ranging from producers, <u>which are at the bottom</u>, to apex predators, <u>which occupy the highest rank</u>. As can be seen from the graph, producers, **consist mostly of** trees, shrubs, and grass, and primary consumers, **largely made up of herbivores**, such as crickets and locusts feed on the producers for food. Secondary consumers, also **omnivores**, including lizards eat primary consumers. From the information supplied, the following two divisions are **tertiary** consumers and fourth consumers randomly eating small insects and omnivores from the previous rank. Finally, there are apex predators, also the **carnivores**, and the **representative** of the highest rank, such as lions, which have almost zero threats in the natural world.

提供的是兩個圖表（figure a 和 figure b）說明生態金字塔。在 figure a 的階層等級可以區分成六個範疇，範圍從位於底部的生產者到佔據最高階層的頂端掠食者。如圖片所示，生產者大部分是由樹木、灌木和草所組成，而主要消費者大部分是由草食性動物，例如蟋蟀和蝗蟲，以生產者為食的動物。次級消費者，也就是雜食性動物，包含蜥蜴，食用主要消費者。所提供的資訊中，接下來的兩個分層是第三級消費者和第四級消費者，隨機以先前層級中的小型昆蟲和雜食性動物為食。最後是頂端掠食者，也就是肉食性動物，最高層級的代表，例如獅子，在自然界中的威脅近乎是零。

A glance at the figure b provided reveals another aspect of the role of organisms in each hierarchy. Figure b demonstrates a more **simplified** version of the ecological pyramid, which only consists of four categories. The foundation of the ecological pyramid is phytoplankton, and the subsequent categories contain seals and "fish and penguins" respectively. The **pinnacle** of the pyramid is occupied by killer whales, which are apex predators in this ecosystem.

掃視圖表 b 所揭露在每個階層中生物有機體的另外一個面向。圖表 b 展示了生態金字塔的簡化版本，僅僅由四個範疇所組成。生態金字塔底部是浮游生物，而接續的範疇包含了海豹和「魚和企鵝」。金字塔頂端是由殺人鯨所佔據，也就是這個生態系統中的頂級掠食者。

It is **intriguing** to note that there is the percent of energy next to each layer, a remarkable difference from figure a. The producers get a hundred percent energy, but in the next layer, the energy is only 10% left. It is evident from the information provided that there is bound to be a 90 percent energy loss occurring from one layer to the next. The energy loss is unbelievably tremendous, leaving the tertiary animals, such killer whales, retained only **a thousandth** of the energy.

引人注意的是在每個層級旁有著能量的百分比，這點是跟圖表 a 有顯著不同之處。生產者獲得 100%的能量，但是到了下個階層，能量僅剩 10%。從提供的資訊可以明顯看出，從一個階層到下一個階層間有著 90%的能量流失。能量流失之大是令人難以置信的，這使得第三層級的動物，例如殺人鯨僅獲得千分之一的能量。

To sum up, both pyramids represent different concepts of biology, although some parts are correlated. The former one shows the role and relationships from each layer through the realization of the food web, and the latter one is about the energy loss and the scarcity of energy that retains.

總結，兩個金字塔代表著不同的生物學概念，儘管有些部分是相關聯的。前者展示出每個階層的角色和關係，透過食物網的概念來呈現，而後者是關於能量流失和能量稀有性的保存。

NOTE

UNIT 04

三圓餅圖題：
三項飲品在各時段的飲用比例

Writing Task 1

You should spend about 20 minutes on this task

The diagram below includes three pie charts. Each pie chart represents a major drink in Taiwan. The percentage of the consumption of three drinks in four major meals can actually reveal people's habits and preference for drinks in a specific timeframe.

Summarize the information by selecting and reporting the main features, and make comparisons where relevant.

Write at least 150 words

🎓 整合能力強化 ❶ 實際演練

請搭配左頁的題目和下方的圖片進行圖表題寫作的演練。

Percentage of the pearl milk tea, coffee, and green tea in typical meals consumed in Taiwan

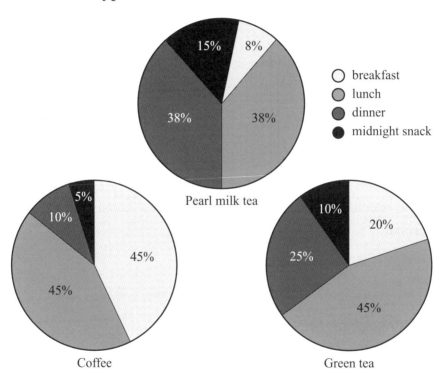

Part 2
雅思寫作 Task1：圖表題小作文

在掌握文法句型後，學習者大多能拿到 7 分以上的寫作成績，英語句型多樣性是獲取高分的關鍵，現在請演練接下來的單句中譯英練習。請務必演練後再觀看答案，也可以搭配範文音檔強化對各句型的記憶。

❶ 在早餐期間，咖啡勝出，有著 45%的大比率，而綠茶有著最低的百分比，僅有 20%的比率。

_____

_____

【參考答案】

During the breakfast, coffee prevails, with a significant 45%, while green tea has the lowest percentage, consisting of only 20 percent.

❷ 引人注目的是在午餐期間，綠茶和咖啡均有著相同比率的消費型態，45%的比率。

_____

_____

【參考答案】

It is intriguing to note that during the lunch, green tea and coffee both have the same portion of consumption, 45%.

❸ 與珍珠奶茶相比較，在早餐期間飲用咖啡的比例比起飲用珍珠奶茶的比例更高。

_____

_____

【參考答案】

Compared with pearl milk tea, the percentage of coffee during the breakfast is immensely greater than that of pearl milk tea.

❹ 在珍珠奶茶的部分，午餐和晚餐有著同樣的消費情形，分別佔有 39%和 38%的比率。

_____

_____

【參考答案】

In the pearl milk tea section, lunch and dinner have identical consumption, respectively having 39% and 38%.

❺ 總之，三個圓餅圖顯示出不僅是數據的百分比，而且是習慣的表現，因為習慣讓一個人所從事的事物和飲用的飲料有著固定的形式。

_____

_____

【參考答案】

To sum up, three pie charts exhibit not only the percentage of figures, but also the habit, since the habit sets the pattern of the day people do and consume.

TOPIC

The diagram below includes three pie charts. Each pie chart represents a major drink in Taiwan. The percentage of the consumption of three drinks in four major meals can actually reveal people's habits and preference for drinks in a specific timeframe.

Summarize the information by selecting and reporting the main features, and make comparisons where relevant.

Step 1　先看題目的圖表題為何種形式，並統一以 **Given is/ are...diagram(s)...**or **A glance at the graph(s)....**等套句開頭，避免使用 the pic shows...等較低階的簡單句型。

Step 2　很快掃描三個圓餅圖後開始構思，重點一定要放在比較相似處和相異處，避免只是一直陳述文句但缺少各個飲品或各飲用時間的比較，這樣分數不會高。

　　■ 先以早餐期間為開頭比較了咖啡和綠茶，而咖啡有了 **a significant 45%**，這是個很好的比較開頭，接續使用了

80

It is intriguing to note，比較了午餐的部分，然後使用很常用的比較慣用語 **compared with**，並使用了 is **immensely** greater than that of pearl milk tea。

■ 最後在同個項目內比較了珍珠奶茶，用到了 **identical** consumption 和 **respectively** having 是很好的表達。

Step 3　次段落使用 **From the information supplied** 這個常見的切入句，在午夜餐點的部分進行比較，運用到了 **remarkably lower**，還有提到一個高階字 **caffeine** 和相關描述豐富了綠茶和咖啡的表達，最後提到在早晨的部分咖啡因扮演的重要角色。

Step 4　最後總結出，這也跟習慣有關，習慣影響一個人的消費行為。

81

經由先前的演練後，現在請看整篇範文並聆聽音檔

A glance at three pie charts provided reveals the average consumption in different meals. During the breakfast, coffee prevails, with a **significant** 45%, while green tea has the lowest percentage, consisting of only 20 percent. It is intriguing to note that during the lunch, green tea and coffee both have the same portion of consumption, 45%. **Compared with** pearl milk tea, the percentage of coffee during the breakfast is **immensely** greater than that of pearl milk tea. In the pearl milk tea section, lunch and dinner have **identical** consumption, **respectively** having 39% and 38%.

掃視所提供的三個圓餅圖揭露在不同餐點中的平均消費。在早餐期間，咖啡勝出，有著大比率的 45%，而綠茶有著最低的百分比，僅有 20%。引人注目的是在午餐期間，綠茶和咖啡均有著相同比例的消費情形，45%的比率。與珍珠奶茶相比較，在早餐期間飲用咖啡的比例比起飲用珍珠奶茶的比例更高。在珍珠奶茶的部分，午餐和晚餐有著同樣的消費情形，分別佔有 39%和 38%的比率。

From the information supplied, in the midnight snack section, coffee and green tea all have **remarkably lower** consumption in their component, perhaps due to the fact that they contain **caffeine**, which **invigorates** the brain, making people harder to fall asleep.

In the morning; however, this is served as the important function so that people go to work with a coffee in hand.

從所提供的資訊中顯示，在午夜的宵夜部分，咖啡和綠茶在他們的組成部分，都有顯著低比例的消費情形，或許是由於他們包含咖啡因，能使大腦活耀，讓人們更難入睡。然而，在早晨，這卻被視為是重要的功能，如此人們去上班時手裡就有杯咖啡。

To sum up, three pie charts exhibit not only the percentage of figures, but also the habit, since **the habit sets the pattern of the day** people do and consume.

總之，三個圓餅圖顯示出不僅是數據的百分比，而且是習慣的表現，因為習慣讓一個人所從事的事物和飲用的飲料有著固定的形式。

柱狀圖題：
四項小遊戲在三個不同年齡層的遊戲次數高低

 Writing Task 1

You should spend about 20 minutes on this task

The diagram below includes four major small games people usually play in Taiwan.

The bar graph measures the frequency, how many times people play, and four major games in three different age groups.

Summarize the information by selecting and reporting the main features, and make comparisons where relevant.

Write at least 150 words

整合能力強化 ❶ 實際演練

請搭配左頁的題目和下方的圖片進行圖表題寫作的演練。

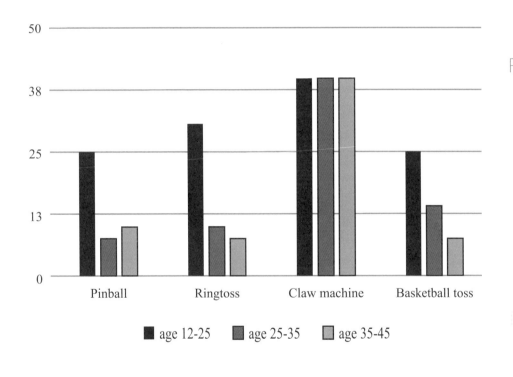

Frequency of small games people play in Taiwan
Four major small games

在掌握文法句型後，學習者大多能拿到 7 分以上的寫作成績，英語句型多樣性是獲取高分的關鍵，現在請演練接下來的單句中譯英練習。請務必演練後再觀看答案，也可以搭配範文音檔強化對各句型的記憶。

❶ 從所提供的資料顯示，夾娃娃機在三個不同的年齡層中有著相同的遊戲次數，而其他三個小遊戲，遊戲次數則不同且有波動。

_____

_____

【參考答案】

From the information supplied, claw machines have the same frequency of playing, 40 times in three various age groups, whereas in other three small games, the frequency of playing varies and fluctuates.

❷ 在彈珠球遊戲中，12-25 歲的遊戲次數為 25 次，但是到了 25-35 歲時有著顯著的跌幅到了僅僅 5 次，然後在 35-45 歲時有些微爬升至 10 次。

_____

_____

【參考答案】

In pinballs, the frequency of playing in age 12-25 has 25 times, but drops significantly to only 5 times in age 25-35, then climbing slightly to 10 times in age 35-45.

❸ 在丟圈圈中，較年輕的世代即 12-25 歲的年齡層中有著最高的遊戲次數，而到了 25-35 歲的年齡層則有了顯著的跌幅來到 10 次，接續在 35-45 歲的年齡層中有著逐步的降幅。

【參考答案】

In ring tosses, the frequency of playing also has the highest among younger groups, in age 12-25, and has an immense descend to 10 times in age 25-35, followed by a gradual decrease in age 35-45.

❹ 引人注目的是在籃球投擲，在較年長的世代中有著最低比率的遊戲次數。

【參考答案】

It is intriguing to note that in basketball tosses, the frequency of playing also has lowest rates of playing among older generations.

❺ 人們越年長，越少人玩籃球投擲的小遊戲，因為它需要體力。

【參考答案】

The older people get, the less people play basketball toss, a game that requires physical stamina.

TOPIC

The diagram below includes four major small games people usually play in Taiwan.

The bar graph measures the frequency, how many times people play, and four major games in three different age groups.

Summarize the information by selecting and reporting the main features, and make comparisons where relevant.

Step 1　先看題目的圖表題為何種形式,並統一以 **Given is/ are...diagram(s)...**or **A glance at the graph(s)...**等套句開頭,避免使用 the pic shows...等較低階的簡單句型。

Step 2　接著看下圖表中有四個小遊戲、玩遊戲的次數和三個主要年齡層,然後開始構思,重點一樣放在比較異同處,使用切入句 **From the information supplied**,先看娃娃機的部分和其他三項小遊戲的比較,並運用到兩個關鍵動詞 varies and **fluctuates**。

Step 3　依序看玩彈珠、套圈圈和投籃球的部分。玩彈珠用到了 has 25 times, but **drops significantly** to only 5 times in age 25-35, then **climbing slightly** to 10 times in age 35-45.（很流暢的表達可以記下來）。在套圈圈的部分則用到 **an immense descend** to 10 times in age 25-35, followed by **a gradual decrease** in age 35-45.。（要注意時態和形容詞子句的省略）。最後以 It is **intriguing** to note 表達投籃球的部分，描述到人們越年長越缺乏精力在這個小遊戲上。

Step 4　最後以娃娃機的部分總結，提到了娃娃機的流行度和跨年齡層的受歡迎層度，用到了 **transcends** all three age groups, **remaining remarkably constant**，可以將這些用法記下。

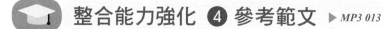

經由先前的演練後，現在請看整篇範文並聆聽音檔

Given is a diagram about four major small games people play in Taiwan and with three different age groups. **From the information supplied**, claw machines have the same frequency of playing, 40 times in three various age groups, whereas in other three small games, the frequency of playing varies and **fluctuates**. In pinballs, the frequency of playing in age 12-25 has 25 times, but **drops significantly** to only 5 times in age 25-35, then **climbing slightly** to 10 times in age 35-45. In ring tosses, the frequency of playing also has the highest among younger groups, in age 12-25, and has **an immense descend** to 10 times in age 25-35, followed by **a gradual decrease** in age 35-45. It is **intriguing** to note that in basketball tosses, the frequency of playing also has lowest rates of playing among older generations. The older people get, the less people play basketball toss, a game that requires physical stamina.

提供的是一個圖表說明人們在台灣玩的四個主要的小遊戲且區分成三個年齡組成。從所提供的資料顯示，夾娃娃機在三個不同的年齡層中有著相同的遊戲次數，而在其他三個小遊戲，遊戲次數則不同且有波動。在彈珠球遊戲中，在 12-25 歲的遊戲的次數為 25 次，但是到了 25-35 歲時有著顯著的跌幅到了僅僅 5 次，然後在 35-45 歲時，些微爬升至 10 次。在丟圈圈中，在較年輕的世代即 12-25 歲的年齡層中有著最高的遊戲次數，而到了 25-35 歲的年齡層有了顯著的跌幅來到 10 次，接續在 35-45 歲的年齡層中有著逐步的降幅。引人興趣注目的是在籃球投擲，在較年長的世代中有著最低比率的遊戲次數。人們越年長，越少人玩籃球投擲的小遊戲，因為其需要身體的精力。

In conclusion, the claw machine **transcends** all three age groups, **remaining remarkably constant** in the number of times people play, 40 times. The popularity of the claw machine makes it a game not only suitable for all age groups, but also **triumphs** the other three small games.

總之，娃娃機跨越了三個年齡層，驚人地維持在人們玩小遊戲的次數 40 次。娃娃機的流行程度讓它不僅僅是適於所有年齡層，而且在其他三個小遊戲中勝出。

UNIT 06

流程圖題：
湖泊消長的四個階段圖

Writing Task 1

You should spend about 20 minutes on this task

The diagram below shows four stages of the lake. From the beginning of the lake, figure a to figure d, after encountering the succession. The lake goes through processes (A-D) and eventually has become a static, nonfluid, dead lake.

Summarize the information by selecting and reporting the main features, and make comparisons where relevant.

Write at least 150 words

整合能力強化 **❶ 實際演練**

請搭配左頁的題目和下方的圖片進行圖表題寫作的演練。

Aquatic Succession

Lake A

Lake B

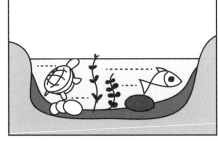

Lake C

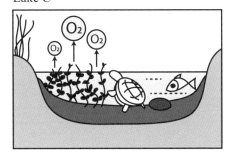

Lake D

在掌握文法句型後，學習者大多能拿到 7 分以上的寫作成績，英語句型多樣性是獲取高分的關鍵，現在請演練接下來的單句中譯英練習。請務必演練後再觀看答案，也可以搭配範文音檔強化對各句型的記憶。

❶ 湖泊是短暫的，而大多數的時候它們會經歷幾個階段的變化而死亡。

_____

_____

【參考答案】

Lakes are ephemeral, and most of the time they will go through several stages of changes and die.

❷ 湖泊演進的過程就稱為湖泊消長。有時候這個現象和水質優養化有關。

_____

_____

【參考答案】

The processes of the progression of a lake are called lake succession. Sometimes the phenomenon of eutrophication is involved.

❸ 雨量沖刷掉土地上的沉積物和營養物質。這些物質最終儲藏到湖泊裡。

_____

_____

【參考答案】

Rainfall washes away sediments and nutrients from the land. These materials eventually stash into the lake.

❹ 沉降的物質對於水生植物，例如藻類是個恩賜。

_____

_____

【參考答案】

Submerging materials are a boon to water plants, such algae.

❺ 隨著時間的演進，沉積物使得湖泊的整體大小縮水了，而在湖泊中逐漸滋長的營養物質讓藻類繁盛。

_____

_____

【參考答案】

Throughout the passage of time, sediments make the overall size of the lake shrink, whereas growing nutrients in the lake make algae groom.

Part 1
雅思寫作 Task1 ：精選高分字彙

Part 2
雅思寫作 Task1 ：圖表題小作文

Part 3
雅思寫作 Task2 ：大作文

TOPIC

The diagram below shows four stages of the lake. From the beginning of the lake, figure a to figure d, after encountering the succession. The lake goes through processes (A-D) and eventually has become a static, nonfluid, dead lake.

Summarize the information by selecting and reporting the main features, and make comparisons where relevant.

Step 1　先看題目的圖表題為何種形式，並統一以 **Given is/ are...diagram(s)...** or **A glance at the graph(s)**....等套句開頭，避免使用 the pic shows...等較低階的簡單句型。

Step 2　先看一下圖形的變化，這題較難，可以想下湖泊的變化，運用到短暫的高階形容詞 **ephemeral**。**定義**並表達出這個現象水質優養化有關。The processes of the **progression** of a lake are called lake **succession**. Sometimes the phenomenon of **eutrophication** is involved.

Step 3   接著描述起初湖泊的狀態到變化的部分，用到了 remains **impervious** to 和幾個高階字 **sediments** and **nutrients, stash** 和 **Submerging**。最後提到關鍵的物質水藻。

Step 4   接續構思湖泊接續可能面臨到的變化，幾個變化都導致湖泊的面積又萎縮了，當中運用到幾個高階字 make algae **groom, proportion**, **oxygen**, **living organisms**。然後要想到湖泊漸漸由原先狀態變成沼澤狀態到更加萎縮的狀態，最後面臨死亡。大概主要的變化點都描述到其實就差不多了，可以多注意這類的考題，不會突然遇到時一時之間不知道要怎麼應對。

經由先前的演練後，現在請看整篇範文並聆聽音檔

Given is a diagram about the succession of a lake. Lakes are **ephemeral**, and most of the time they will go through several stages of changes and die. The processes of the **progression** of a lake are called lake **succession**. Sometimes the phenomenon of **eutrophication** is involved.

提供的是一個圖表說明湖泊的消長。湖泊是短暫的，而大多數的時候它們會經歷幾個階段的變化而死亡。湖泊演進的過程就稱為湖泊消長。有時候這個現象和水質優養化有關。

Originally, the lake remains **impervious** to the change and is pretty healthy. （**Lake A**）Rainfall washes away **sediments** and **nutrients** from the land. These materials eventually **stash** into the lake. **Submerging** materials are a boon to water plants, such algae.

起初，湖泊對於改變不為所動而且相當健康。（湖泊 **A**）雨量沖刷土地上的沉積物和營養物質。這些物質最終儲藏到湖泊裡。沉降的物質對於水生植物，例如藻類是個恩賜。

Throughout the passage of time, sediments make the overall size of the lake shrink, whereas growing nutrients in the lake make algae groom. The **proportion** of the lake get even smaller.（**Lake B**）Reeds and grass around the lake also build up. Other species of trees and plants also **take up** the space of the lake. In addition, **algae boom deprives of** the oxygen in the lake, making living organisms harder to live.（**Lake C**）The lake initially a wetland has become a dead one later, with fewer species living and the space shrinking. Ultimately, more sediments **fill in** the lake and the lake dies.（**Lake D**） It has become a land that we see later.

隨著時間的演進，沉積物使得湖泊的整體大小縮水了，而在湖泊中逐漸滋長的營養物質讓藻類繁盛。湖泊的比例甚至變得更小了。（湖泊 B）湖邊的蘆葦和草也建構起來。其他種類的樹木和植物也佔據著湖泊的空間。此外，藻類的繁盛剝奪了湖泊中的氧氣，讓活著的有機體更難生存。（湖泊 C）湖泊起初是個沼澤，於稍後已經變成死亡湖泊，隨著生存的物種更少且空間縮小了。最終，更多的沉積物填入湖泊裡頭，以至於湖泊死亡了。（湖泊 D）這已經成為了我們稍後看到的土地了。

UNIT 01

「小時了了」和「大器晚成」，何者在人生道路上較具有優勢呢？

Writing Task 2 ▶ *MP3 015*

TOPIC

In life, some people have achieved so many in their early years, and we cannot help but think how lucky they are, whereas others (late bloomers) have endured so much and their successes arrive much later than the early bloomers. What do you think about this phenomenon? Which one is better? Discuss both ideas (early bloomers and late bloomers) and give your opinion.

Write at least 250 words

整合能力強化 **1** 實際演練

請搭配左頁的題目和並構思和完成大作文的演練。

_____

_____

_____

_____

_____

_____

_____

_____

_____

_____

_____

_____

_____

_____

_____

_____

Part 3
雅思寫作 **Task2**：大作文

　　在掌握文法句型後，學習者大多能拿到 7 分以上的寫作成績，英語句型多樣性是獲取高分的關鍵，現在請演練接下來的單句中譯英練習。請務必演練後再觀看答案，也可以搭配範文音檔強化對各句型的記憶。

❶ 生命中的贏家不見得總是及早獲取成功者，也就是所謂的「小時了了者」，反而是「大器晚成者」。

_____

_____

【參考答案】

The winner in life does not always be people who succeed early, the so called "early bloomers" but "late bloomers".

❷ 甚至算命師都能察覺出一個人在生命初期的階段是否能獲取成功，或是一個人在他或她最終享受成功的果實前是否可能需要歷經許多迂迴曲折的道路。

_____

_____

【參考答案】

Even fortune tellers can tell whether a person can achieve success in early years of life or whether a person might take lots of detours before he or she can eventually enjoy the fruits of the success.

❸ 算命師所告訴我們的可能是也可能不是全然精確的，但是它向我
們許多人傳達出人們確實在乎他們人生中自我的成功。

_____

_____

【參考答案】

What fortune tellers tell us might or might not be entirely
accurate, but it sends the message to many of us that people do
care about their own success in life.

❹ 有時候人們對於有些人在他或她早期的成年生活中已獲取的成功
感到忌妒，沒有了解到這個現象背後所造成的影響。

_____

_____

【參考答案】

Sometimes people get jealous of someone who has achieved so
much in his or her early adult life without realizing the
repercussions behind the phenomenon.

❺ 在一個人早期的成年生活中就獲取甚鉅是很棒的，但是獲取甚鉅
並不等同於，此成就在所有人生階段中能持續著。

_____

_____

【參考答案】

Achieving so much in one's early adult life is great, but achieving
so much does not equal as lasting the accomplishment throughout
the entire life.

❻ 這就是為什麼我們有句關於人們成功的俗諺：「幸運不可能總是站在你這邊。」

_____

_____

【參考答案】

That is why we have a saying about people's success "you cannot have the luck to be on your side all the time."

❼ 大器晚成者反而比小時小小者更好，許多的年輕成功消失殆盡，而花費餘生悲嘆他們過去所擁有的」。

_____

_____

【參考答案】

It's better to be a late bloomer than an early one; so many young successes flame out and spend the rest of their lives lamenting what they used to have."

❽ 或許你可以在另一很棒的本書《勝利，並非事事順利：30 位典範人物不藏私的人生真心話》中發現類似的想法，史黛西・史奈德提供了她對於成功的洞察。「在好萊塢，有兩種類型的高級主管：光芒燒的炙熱但很快消失殆盡，和有著長遠、令人感到有趣且強而有力的職涯。

_____

_____

104

【參考答案】

Or you can find another similar concept in another great book, *Getting There*. In "*Getting There*", Stacey Snider offers her insight about success. "In Hollywood, there are two kinds of executives: The flames that burn brightly and quickly go out and the executives who have long, interesting, and powerful careers.

❾ 而我選擇成為後者中的其中一員。」而且，許多關於人們在人生初期獲取甚鉅，卻在他們較晚期的成年生活中過得相當糟的故事。

_____

_____

【參考答案】

I aspired to be one of the latter." Also, numerous stories about people who have achieved so much in early life end up pretty bad in their later adult life.

❿ 成功得來的太容易了而有時候僅僅是因為幸運。他們似乎無法駕馭或珍惜他們生活中所獲得的。

_____

_____

【參考答案】

Successes have come too quick and sometimes it is merely out of luck. They cannot seem to harness or cherish what they have gotten in their life.

TOPIC

In life, some people have achieved so many in their early years, and we cannot help but think how lucky they are, whereas others (late bloomers) have endured so much and their successes arrive much later than the early bloomers. What do you think about this phenomenon? Which one is better? Discuss both ideas (early bloomers and late bloomers) and give your opinion.

搭配的暢銷書

- *Mistakes I Made at Work*《我在工作中所犯的錯誤》
- *Getting There*《勝利，並非事事順利：30 位典範人物不藏私的人生真心話》

Step 1　題目是詢問關於小時了了和大器晚成，可以先構思所要選定的立場為何，範文中提到的是「**大器晚成**」較佳。（如果要選擇小時小小較佳，可以先列出幾個優點再進行兩者間的比較。）首段可以先定義並簡述兩者，接著描述出算命師預測一個人的運勢，包含了兩者，但也非全然反映出全貌，因為當中還牽涉到個人努力等等。

106

Step 2 　　次段描述到小時了了則受到忌妒，並表達出小時了了的成
就並不代表永恆，確實運勢有可能是「十年河東，十年河
西」，大器晚成者更不需要枉自菲薄（像姜子牙即是代
表）。最後描述到幸運和運勢。

Step 3 　　下個段落描述到兩本暢銷書的論點《我在工作中所犯的錯
誤》和《勝利，並非事事順利：30 位典範人物不藏私的人
生真心話》，兩本均表達出相似的論點，早期獲取的成功
像火焰般，燃燒的炙烈但也很快就消失殆盡。這點很值得
深省，另外還提到了，當成功得到的太容易時，人容易迷
失且不懂得珍惜。（這在新聞中可以常看到，確實是個借
鏡。）

Step 4 　　末段，根據先前段落的論述中推論出「大器晚成」較小時
了了佳。

Part 1
雅思寫作 Task1：精選高分字彙

Part 2
雅思寫作 Task1：圖表題小作文

Part 3
雅思寫作 Task2：大作文

經由先前的演練後，現在請看整篇範文並聆聽音檔

The concept of early bloomers and late bloomers has been an ongoing debate for generations after generations. The winner in life does not always be people who succeed early, the so called "early bloomers" but "late bloomers". Even fortune tellers can tell whether a person can achieve success in early years of life or whether a person might take lots of detours before he or she can eventually enjoy the fruits of the success. What fortune tellers tell us might or might not be entirely accurate, but it sends the message to many of us that people do care about their own success in life.

小時了了和大器晚成的觀念一直是世世代代間不斷爭論的議題。生命中的贏家不見得總是及早獲取成功者，也就是所謂的「小時了了者」，反而是「大器晚成者」。甚至算命師都能察覺出一個人在生命初期的階段是否能獲取成功，或是一個人在他或她最終享受成功的果實前是否可能需要歷經許多迂迴曲折的道路。算命師所告訴我們的可能是，也可能不是全然精確的，但是它向我們許多人傳達出人們確實在乎他們人生中自我的成功。

Sometimes people get jealous of someone who has achieved so much in his or her early adult life without realizing the repercussions behind the phenomenon. Achieving so much in one's early adult life is great, but achieving so much does not equal as lasting the accomplishment throughout the entire life. That is why we have a saying about people's success "you cannot have the luck to be on your side all the time." The wheel of the luck might be turning into other people when it is their turn to be lucky.

有時候人們對於有些人在他或她早期的成年生活中已獲取的成功感到忌妒，沒有了解到這個現象背後所造成的影響。在一個人早期的成年生活中就獲取甚鉅是很棒的，但是獲取甚鉅並不等同於，此成就在所有人生階段中能持續著。這就是為什麼我們有句關於人們成功的俗諺：「幸運不可能總是站在你這邊。」幸運之輪可能轉向其他人，當該是那些人該獲取幸運的時候。

In "*Mistakes I Made at Work*", Ruth Reichl shares her tips about success. "Don't expect too much of yourself when you're young. It's better to be a late bloomer than an early one; so many young successes flame out and spend the rest of their lives lamenting what they used to have." Or you can find another similar concept in another great book, *Getting There*. In "*Getting There*", Stacey Snider offers her insight about success. "In Hollywood, there are two kinds of executives: The flames that burn brightly and quickly go out and the executives who have long, interesting, and powerful careers. I aspired to be one of the latter." Also, numerous stories about people who have achieved so much in early life end up pretty bad in their later adult life. Successes have come too quick and sometimes it is merely out of luck. They cannot seem to harness or cherish what they have gotten in their life.

在《我在工作中所犯的錯誤》，露絲・瑞奇分享她關於成功的秘訣。「當你年輕時，別對自己有太高的要求。大器晚成者反而比小時小小者更好，許多的年輕成功消失殆盡，而花費餘生悲嘆他們過去所擁有的」。或許你可以在另一很棒的本書《勝利，並非事事順利：30 位典範人物不藏私的人生真心話》中發現類似的想法，史黛西・史奈德提供了她對於成功的洞察。

「在好萊塢，有兩種類型的高級主管：光芒燒的炎熱但很快消失殆盡，和有著長遠、令人感到有趣且強而有力的職涯。而我選擇成為後者中的其中一員。」而且，許多關於人們在人生初期獲取甚鉅，卻在他們較晚期的成年生活中過得相當糟的故事。成功得來的太容易了而有時候僅僅是因為幸運。他們似乎無法駕馭或珍惜他們生活中所獲得的。

To sum up, for all these reasons, I am in favor of the idea that being a later bloomer is better than being an early one, since you have to endure so many hardships to realize the value of success and therefore cherish it.

總之，基於這些原因，我認同當個大器晚成者比小時了了者更佳的想法，因為你必須要忍受許多艱難才能體會到成功的價值，並因此感到珍惜它。

UNIT
02

畢業後面臨就業，你會選擇
「藍領工作」還是「白領工
作」，為什麼呢？

Writing Task 2 ▶ *MP3 017*

TOPIC

Nowadays, lower wages are prevalent among younger generations, and statistics has shown that blue collar jobs offer job applicants significantly higher salaries than white collar jobs. However, it seems that higher salaries are not the top concern among graduates because there are other considerations. Which job will you choose, a blue collar job or a white collar job? Use specific examples and give your opinion.

Write at least 250 words

整合能力強化 **1** 實際演練

請搭配左頁的題目和並構思和完成大作文的演練。

_____

_____

_____

_____

_____

_____

_____

_____

_____

_____

_____

_____

_____

_____

_____

_____

113

　　在掌握文法句型後，學習者大多能拿到 7 分以上的寫作成績，英語句型多樣性是獲取高分的關鍵，現在請演練接下來的單句中譯英練習。請務必演練後再觀看答案，也可以搭配範文音檔強化對各句型的記憶。

❶ 根據統計，許多人選擇了白領的工作而非選擇藍領的工作，即使相較之下，藍領工作的薪資比起白領工作更高。

_____

_____

【參考答案】

According to the statistics, lots of people are choosing white-collar jobs instead of picking blue-collar jobs, even if comparatively the salary of the blue-collar jobs is much higher than that of white collar jobs.

❷ 所進行的調查結果並沒有令許多專家和學者們感到驚訝，因為藍領工作牽涉到許多艱困的工作和勞力。

_____

_____

【參考答案】

The survey conducted does not astound many experts and scholars since blue-collar jobs involve some arduous work and labor.

❸ 較年輕的世代，不像較年長的世代，那種會願意從事任何工作只要利益勝於其他工作，將乾淨和舒適感列於薪資更前端。

_____

_____

【參考答案】

Younger generations, unlike older generations, who will do whatever it takes as long as the benefit outweighs the other, put the cleanliness and comfort much ahead of the salary.

❹ 上述的陳述可能並非以精準的方式去呈現兩方的立場，但是你越早工作，你越能了解到你所喜歡從事的工作。

_____

_____

【參考答案】

The above statements might not be an accurate way to present both sides, but the earlier you work, the earlier you will figure out what you like to do.

❺ 有些白領工作者，在公司工作幾年後，最終了解到藍領工作才是他們嚮往的。

_____

_____

【參考答案】

Some white-collar workers after working in the office for a few years, eventually figure out that blue-collar jobs are what they

Part 1
雅思寫作 Task1：精選高分字彙

Part 2
雅思寫作 Task1：圖表題小作文

Part 3
雅思寫作 Task2：大作文

fancy.

❻ 其他人像是傑瑞・卡布納里在《第一份工作》中最終了解到藍領工作不是一份他將來想從事的工作，在他具有芝加哥的魚公司工作經驗後。

_____

_____

【參考答案】
Others like Jerry Carbonari in "*First Jobs*" eventually figures out the blue-collar job is not the job that he will be doing after his job experiences in a fish company in Chicago.

❼ 依我來看，我在高中時已經從事了許多的藍領工作。對於那些工作沒有任何浪漫情節在了。

_____

_____

【參考答案】
In my opinion, I have done lots of blue-collar jobs in high school. There was not any romance in such jobs.

❽ 所有那個時期所從事的工作都需要你從事艱苦和耗費勞力的工作，而且即使是不需要耗費體力活的工作，它磨掉了你的耐心。

_____

_____

【參考答案】

All require you to do arduous and strenuous work, and even if it is not something that needs physical work, it wears off your patience.

❾ 最重要的是，當你還相當年輕時，你的身體可以承受那樣的殘酷和工作量，但是當你漸漸年長後，你很難從事那樣的工作。

_____

_____

【參考答案】

Most important of all, when you are really young, your body can afford such cruelty and workload, but when you are getting older, it is highly unlikely for you to do such a job.

❿ 而且，你沒有辦法從工作中累積工作經驗，因為你只是不斷重複做同樣的事情。在大部分的藍領工作做十年後，對於雇主來說仍然意謂著沒什麼重要性，但是當你在從事特定的白領工作時，你能夠累積你的工作經驗。

_____

_____

【參考答案】

Also, you are not going to accumulate work experiences because you are doing the same thing over and over. Ten years of working in most blue-collar jobs still mean nothing to employers in other companies, but when you are doing certain white-collar jobs, you can accumulate your work experiences.

TOPIC

Nowadays, lower wages are prevalent among younger generations, and statistics has shown that blue collar jobs offer job applicants significantly higher salaries than white collar jobs. However, it seems that higher salaries are not the top concern among graduates because there are other considerations. Which job will you choose, a blue collar job or a white collar job? Use specific examples and give your opinion.

搭配的暢銷書

■ *First Jobs*《第一份工作》

Step 1　題目是詢問關於兩種類型的工作：在白領工作和藍領工作中的選擇。首段以清楚且流暢的表達來呈現，包含兩者間的比較，並談到兩個世代在選擇上的不同，最後以年輕世代的考量點（**乾淨和舒適感**）作結尾。

Step 2　次個段落，除了延續上個段落的陳述外，包含了工作者在工作選擇上的改變，由白領到藍領（代表年輕世代並非都

會持續選擇白領工作）。接續以暢銷書《第一份工作》進行論述，作者有了在芝加哥的魚公司工作體驗後，更了解自己想要什麼，進而不想選擇藍領工作。（確實有實際的工作體驗後，更能協助了解自我，而各種因素都影響了人選擇藍領或白領工作，也代表並沒有絕對要選擇哪樣的工作，這個並無是非對錯）。

Step 3　末段拉回自己本身的工作體驗，當中描述到藍領工作的辛苦處等等，最主要的論點是放在為什麼選擇藍領或白領工作，範文中選擇的論點是會想選擇「白領工作」，必須要有支持這方面的特點或原因在，文中也陸續提到了，藍領工作很難累積工作經驗，因為工作的重複性太高，也代表取代性高，另一方面是這是勞力工作，在年輕時體力能夠負擔，但是之後卻不見得能夠如此。

Step 4　經由前幾個段落的論述後，末段表明出自己仍會選擇白領工作。

Part 1
雅思寫作 Task1：精選高分字彙

Part 2
雅思寫作 Task1：圖表題小作文

Part 3
雅思寫作 Task2：大作文

經由先前的演練後，現在請看整篇範文並聆聽音檔

According to the statistics, lots of people are choosing white-collar jobs instead of picking blue-collar jobs, even if comparatively the salary of the blue-collar jobs is much higher than that of white-collar jobs. The survey conducted does not astound many experts and scholars since blue-collar jobs involve some arduous work and labor. Younger generations, unlike older generations, who will do whatever it takes as long as the benefit outweighs the other, put the cleanliness and comfort much ahead of the salary.

根據統計，許多人選擇了白領的工作而非選擇藍領的工作，即使相較之下，藍領工作的薪資比起白領工作更高。所進行的調查結果並沒有令許多專家和學者們感到驚訝，因為藍領工作牽涉到許多艱困的工作和勞力。較年輕的世代，不像較年長的世代，那種會願意從事任何工作只要利益勝於其他工作，將乾淨和舒適感列於薪資更前端。

The above statements might not be an accurate way to present both sides, but the earlier you work, the earlier you will figure out what you like to do. Some white-collar workers after working in the office for a few years, eventually figure out that blue-collar jobs are what they fancy. Others like Jerry Carbonari in "*First Jobs*" eventually figures out the blue-collar job is not the job that he will be doing after his job experiences in a fish company in Chicago. Of course, there are no right or wrong when it comes to choosing the job.

上述的陳述可能並非以精準的方式去呈現兩方的立場，但是你越早工作，你越能了解到你所喜歡從事的工作。有些白領工作者，在公司工作幾年後，最終了解到藍領工作才是他們嚮往的。其他人像是傑瑞‧卡布納里在《第一份工作》中最終了解到藍領工作不是一份他將來想從事的工作，在他具有芝加哥的魚公司工作經驗後。當然，當提到選擇工作時，沒有所謂的對或錯的答案。

In my opinion, I have done lots of blue-collar jobs in high school. There was not any romance in such jobs. All require you to do arduous and strenuous work, and even if it is not something that needs physical work, it wears off your patience. All jobs are repetitive and after those experiences I admire blue-collar workers even more. Those jobs do involve labors and you cannot have any voice. No one would do such a job and people doing those jobs are really for a living. Most important of all, when you are really young, your body can afford such cruelty and workload, but when you are getting older, it is highly unlikely for you to do such a job. Also, you are not going to accumulate work experiences because you are doing the same thing over and over. Ten years of working in most blue-collar jobs still mean nothing to employers in other companies, but when you are doing certain white-collar jobs, you can accumulate your work experiences. You make a job hop after working in the company for 3-5 years, and you are getting a new job title or even get a managerial position that makes your pay double.

依我來看，我在高中時已經從事了許多的藍領工作。對於那些工作沒有任何浪漫情節在了。所有那個時期所從事的工作都需要你從事艱苦和耗費勞力的工作，而且即使是不需要耗費體力活的工作，它磨掉了你的耐心。所有工作都是重複性質的，而在那些工作經驗後，我更欽佩藍領工作者。那些工作牽涉到勞力，以及你不能有任何想法。沒人會想從事那樣的工作，而且人們做那些工作通常是為了生活。最重要的是，當你還相當年輕時，你的身體可以承受那樣的殘酷和工作量，但是當你漸漸年長後，你很難從事那樣的工作。而且，你沒有辦法從工作中累積工作經驗，因為你只是不斷重複做同樣的事情。在大部分的藍領工作做十年後，對於雇主來說仍然意謂著沒什麼重要性，但是當你在從事特定的白領工作時，你能夠累積你的工作經驗。你能夠在公司工作 3 到 5 年後轉職，而且你能獲得新的工作頭銜或是甚至獲取能使你工作薪資兩倍的管理工作。

To sum up, for all these reasons, I think I will choose a white-collar job right after I graduate.

總之，基於這些理由，我認為我在畢業後會選擇白領工作。

升職加薪後你會如何運用那筆
錢呢？是用於犒賞家人來趟國
際旅行還是存起來或投資呢？

Writing Task 2 ▶ *MP3 019*

TOPIC

Without the knowledge about money, money is soon gone. People upgrade their lifestyle when they get promoted or whenever they get bonuses or raises, but wrong ideas of money has put numerous people into a vicious cycle, even top earners in the statistics. What is your opinion about this phenomenon? Use specific examples to illustrate this phenomenon.

Write at least 250 words

整合能力強化 ❶ 實際演練

請搭配左頁的題目和並構思和完成大作文的演練。

125

在掌握文法句型後，學習者大多能拿到 7 分以上的寫作成績，英語句型多樣性是獲取高分的關鍵，現在請演練接下來的單句中譯英練習。請務必演練後再觀看答案，也可以搭配範文音檔強化對各句型的記憶。

❶ 財務知識是一門在學校該被列為是必修課程的，既然大多數的人都對於金錢沒有很清楚的想法。大多數的時候，並不是你所賺取的金錢總額。

_____

_____

【參考答案】

Financial literacy is something that should be taught in school as a required course since most people do not have a clear idea about money. Most of the time, it is not the amount of the money that you earn.

❷ 當然，人們有權將他們的金錢以任何他們想要的方式來使用，但是當提到保存金錢和充份利用時，大多數的人仍有很長的一段路要走。

_____

_____

【參考答案】

Of course, people have the right to spend their money in whatever they want, but when it comes to keeping the money and making the most of it, most people still have a long way to go.

❸ 偶爾你覺得你有股衝動想要寵寵自己只是那麼一些些，而你認為這是無傷大雅的，尤其是當你獲得升遷或有了加薪。

_____

_____

【參考答案】

Every now and then you feel the urge to pamper yourselves just a little bit and you deem that there is no harm in that, especially after you get promoted or have the raise.

❹ 人們將他們的生活方式升級去順應他們增加的收入，但他們卻也陷入陷阱中。

_____

_____

【參考答案】

People upgrade their lifestyle to measure up their increased earnings, but they are also falling into the trap.

❺ 在《勝利，並非事事順利：30 位典範人物不藏私的人生真心話》中，史黛西 史奈德，前環球影城董事長，述說了她第一年在律師事務所非常高額的薪資，但是她想要避免陷入這樣的陷阱中。

_____

_____

Part 1
雅思寫作 Task1：精選高分字彙

Part 2
雅思寫作 Task1：圖表題小作文

Part 3
雅思寫作 Task2：大作文

In *Getting There*, Stacey Snider, a previous Chairman of Universal, states the fact that her first-year salaries at law firms were incredibly high, but she wanted to avoid that kind of trap.

❻ 人們生活的提升迫使他們必須要保有那份工作,即使他們討厭那份工作,以維持他們現有的開銷。

_____

_____

People advancing their living have to keep their jobs, even if they hate the job, to maintain their current spending. Furthermore, in the long term, it is not wise for one's financial planning.

❼ 在《原來有錢人都這麼做》中,作者湯瑪斯 史丹利和威廉 丹柯也警告著,「一個人若賺錢是為了能花費。當你需要花更多錢時,你需要賺取更多。」

_____

_____

That is why In *The Millionaire Next Door*, authors, Thomas J. Stanley and William D. Danko also caution "one earns to spend. When you need to spend more, you need to earn more".

❽ 這也是為什麼在《窮爸爸富爸爸》,它述說到「更多的金錢並不

能解決問題」。

_____

_____

【參考答案】

That is also why in *Rich Dad Poor Dad*, it says "more money won't solve the problem."

❾ 既然人們認為他們有更多的錢，他們浪費掉，認為他們從下次的薪資中拿到錢，但是他們卻未曾想到其他問題。

_____

_____

【參考答案】

Since people think they are having more money, they squander it, thinking they are going to get it in the next paycheck, but they are unaware of other problems.

❿ 金錢從他們的指縫間流掉了。

_____

_____

【參考答案】

Money slips through their fingers.

TOPIC

Without the knowledge about money, money is soon gone. People upgrade their lifestyle when they get promoted or whenever they get bonuses or raises, but wrong ideas of money has put numerous people into a vicious cycle, even top earners in the statistics. What is your opinion about this phenomenon? Use specific examples to illustrate this phenomenon.

搭配的暢銷書

- *Getting There*《勝利，並非事事順利：30 位典範人物不藏私的人生真心話》
- *The Millionaire Next Door*《原來有錢人都這麼做》
- *Rich Dad Poor Dad*《窮爸爸富爸爸》

Step 1　題目是提到若缺乏財務知識，金錢很快就流逝掉了，人們提高自我生活方式和消費是主因。首段描述到，這與所賺的金錢總額無關，而是需要有相對的財務知識去管理金錢，而缺乏此概念導致人們還有很長一段路要走。

Step 2　次個段落提到，在軟體的頁面上的炫耀也是加劇此情況的原因。生活方式的升級更是導致此情況的主因，這是個惡性循環。

- 接著以三本暢銷書連續論述此論點。《勝利，並非事事順利：30 位典範人物不藏私的人生真心話》提到要免於落入陷阱。

- 《原來有錢人都這麼做》提到為了花費而花，則要賺取更多的金錢。最後以《窮爸爸富爸爸》的論點結尾，確實給予一個人更多金錢並不能解決問題。

- 當有錢時，其實必須要維持本來的生活型態。但對大多數的人而言，給予更多錢，就會認為自己值得過到某種程度的生活模式（例如，既然這個月有這麼多錢，那也該來趟歐洲旅遊，住五星級飯店等等），進而也可能是花光錢，等同於本來低薪時也是不夠花或將近月光的生活（所以更多錢並不能解決問題）。

Step 3　末段提到了遵從暢銷書作者或我們祖先的忠告，呼應前面的論述，他們的人生智慧就是累積財富跟降低煩惱之道，仍舊維持同樣的生活水準，他們不會花一分錢在奢侈品上。

（當然這個論點跟活在當下者的論點是大相逕庭的，考生也可以寫反對此論點的立場，並以幾個特點支持相關論述）。

131

經由先前的演練後，現在請看整篇範文並聆聽音檔

Financial literacy is something that should be taught in school as a required course since most people do not have a clear idea about money. Most of the time, it is not the amount of the money that you earn. Of course, people have the right to spend their money in whatever they want, but when it comes to keeping the money and making the most of it, most people still have a long way to go.

財務知識是一門在學校該被列為是必修課程的，既然大多數的人都對於金錢沒有很清楚的想法。大多數的時候，並不是你所賺取的金錢總額。當然，人們有權將他們的金錢以任何他們想要的方式來使用，但是當提到保存金錢和充份利用時，大多數的人仍有很長的一段路要走。

Nowadays, with Facebook, IG and many other apps, you can easily see people brag about fancy stuffs or trips they have taken in those pages, and there is nothing wrong with money spent on fancy trips. Every now and then you feel the urge to pamper yourselves just a little bit and you deem that there is no harm in that, especially after you get promoted or have the raise. People upgrade their lifestyle to measure up their increased earnings, but they are also falling into the trap. In *Getting There*, Stacey Snider, a previous Chairman of Universal, states the fact that her first-year salaries at law firms were incredibly high, but she wanted to avoid that kind of trap. People advancing their living have to keep their jobs, even if they hate the job, to maintain their current spending. Furthermore, in the long term, it is not wise for one's financial planning. That is why In *The Millionaire Next Door*, authors, Thomas J. Stanley and William D. Danko also caution "one earns to spend. When you need to spend more, you need to earn more". So there is another problem. That is also why in *Rich Dad Poor Dad*, it says "more money won't solve the problem." Since people think they are having more money, they squander it, thinking they are going to get it in the next paycheck, but they are unaware of other problems. Money slips through their fingers.

現今，隨著臉書、IG 和許多其他軟體，你可以輕易地在那些頁面中看到人們炫耀華麗的東西或是他們去過的旅行，而花費金錢在豪華旅途上沒有任何不對。偶爾你覺得你有股衝動想要寵寵自己只是那麼一些些，而你認為這是無傷大雅的，尤其是當你獲得升遷或有了加薪。人們將他們的生活方式升級去順應他們增加的收入，但他們卻也陷入陷阱中。在《勝利，並非事事順利：30 位典範人物不藏私的人生真心話》中，史黛西 史奈德，前環球影城董事長，述說了她第一年在律師事務所非常高額的薪資，但是她想要避免陷入這樣的陷阱中。人們生活的提升迫使他們必須要保有那份工作，即使他們討厭那份工作，以維持他們現有的開銷。在《原來有錢人都這麼做》中，作者湯瑪斯 史丹利和威廉 丹柯也警告著，「一個人若賺錢是為了能花費。當你需要花更多錢時，你需要賺取更多。」所以這有著另一個問題。這也是為什麼在《窮爸爸富爸爸》，它述說到「更多的金錢並不能解決問題」。既然人們認為他們有更多的錢，他們浪費掉，認為他們可以從下次的薪資中拿到錢，但是他們卻未曾想到其他問題。金錢從他們的指縫間流掉了。

To sum up, since "money without financial intelligence is money soon gone", I won't squander the money on international trips and many other things, and instead will follow the advice of bestselling authors or our ancestors. Our ancestors are wise enough to say even if their paychecks double because of the raise, they still maintain the same living standard, and they won't spend a dime on other luxuries. That's the only way to keep the money and accumulate the fortune.

總之，既然「有錢但沒有財務知識代表著金錢很快流失掉」，我不會將金錢浪費在國際旅遊和許多事情上，而取而代之的是遵從暢銷書作者或我們祖先的忠告。我們祖先睿智到足以述說著，即使他們的薪資因為加薪而所得變成雙倍，他們仍舊維持同樣的生活水準，他們不會花一分錢在奢侈品上。這就是唯一能保留金錢和累積財富之道。

在求職中「幸運」扮演什麼角色，又該如何表現並增進自己的幸運呢？

Writing Task 2 ▶ *MP3 021*

TOPIC

Most graduates have a wrong idea about job-search, deeming certificates and great resumes can be the cure for their job-finding, but the point is you still have to pass the written and several interviews to get the job offer. Sometimes there are other factors, such as personality and luck. Do you think luck actually plays a role in the job search? Use specific examples to explain.

Write at least 250 words

整合能力強化 ❶ 實際演練

請搭配左頁的題目和並構思和完成大作文的演練。

_____

_____

_____

_____

_____

_____

_____

_____

_____

_____

_____

_____

_____

_____

_____

_____

_____

_____

Part 3
雅思寫作 Task2：大作文

在掌握文法句型後，學習者大多能拿到 7 分以上的寫作成績，英語句型多樣性是獲取高分的關鍵，現在請演練接下來的單句中譯英練習。請務必演練後再觀看答案，也可以搭配範文音檔強化對各句型的記憶。

❶ 許多畢業生誤解了，列出證照和有亮麗的學歷對於他們找工作就足夠了，但是這僅是對於初次篩選。

_____

_____

【參考答案】

Most graduates misconstrue that listing several certificates and having a fancy degree are enough for their job search, but it is just for the first screening.

❷ 在其中一本暢銷書中，《關鍵十年》，它導正了面試者們的觀念。「履歷僅是清單，而清單一點都不引人注目」。

_____

_____

【參考答案】

In one of the bestsellers, *The Defining Decade*, it sets interviewees straight. "Resumes are just lists, and lists are not compelling."

❸ 那些列於履歷表上的成就僅能讓人事專員感到有興趣或是達到主要的標準。面試者仍需要經歷過筆試和幾次的面試才能獲得錄取通知。

_____

_____

【參考答案】

Those accomplishments listed on the resume only get HR personnel intrigued or meet the major criteria. Interviewees still need to go through the written and several interviews to get the offer.

❹ 在這些過程中，任何事情都可能發生，而雇用比我們想像中更為複雜。有著眾多因素會影響一個人如何獲得錄取通知，包含幸運。

_____

_____

【參考答案】

During these processes, anything can happen, and hiring can be more complicated than we imagine. There are multiple factors that will influence how one gets hired, including luck.

❺ 在《幸運如何發生》，高盛公司的總經理說到「你必須要擁有幸運才能拿到工作」，而這是千真萬確的，幸運確實在一個人能否獲取一份工作中扮演了重大的角色。

_____

_____

In *"How Luck Happens"*, the managing director at Goldman Sachs said that "you are going to need luck to get a job", and it is true that luck does play a huge role in whether a person will get the job or not.

❻ 如同通常我們常聽到其他人說的「創造屬於你自己的幸運」。大多數的畢業生卻不知道要從何下手，做點事比起什麼事都不做好多了。

_____

_____

As we often hear what others say "create your own luck". Most graduates just don't know how, doing something is better than doing nothing.

❼ 在《慾望師奶》第一季，湯姆讚美了校長桌上的一張船的相片，儘管這個舉動並沒有打動校長（至少他做了些什麼）。

_____

_____

In *Desperate Housewives*, season 1, Tom compliments the picture of the boat on the principal's table, although doing this does not move the principal. (at least he does something)

❽ 在《成功的方程式》，作者讚美高階主管對於垃圾桶的品味。

_____

_____

【參考答案】

In *The Success Equation*, the author accolades the executive's taste in trash cans.

❾ 幸運確實站在他那邊，而在稍後，其中一位領導人告訴他「有六位面試官在雇用時對你投下了反對票」，但是「主要決策者的決定壓過了他們的評估並堅持我們要錄用你」。

_____

_____

【參考答案】

Luck does work in his favor, and later one of the leaders told him "the six interviewers voted against hiring you", but "the head guy overrode their assessment and insisted we bring you in."

❿ 幸運也可以是你所散發出的個性和魅力。

_____

_____

【參考答案】

Luck can also be the personality and charm that you exude.

TOPIC

Most graduates have a wrong idea about job-search, deeming certificates and great resumes can be the cure for their job-finding, but the point is you still have to pass the written and several interviews to get the job offer. Sometimes there are other factors, such as personality and luck. Do you think luck actually plays a role in the job search? Use specific examples to explain.

搭配的暢銷書

- *The Defining Decade*《關鍵十年》
- *How Luck Happens*《幸運如何發生》
- *The Success Equation*《成功的方程式》

Step 1　題目是詢問在許多的求職準備上，「幸運」是否也扮演了錄取與否的角色，這個題目蠻有特色，但也比較難發揮，範文中融入了幾本暢銷書，讓文章看起來更有趣且有論點支持幸運確實扮演了錄取與否的角色。

- 首段先以暢銷書《關鍵十年》導正面試者的想法，因為對大多數畢業生來說，並未求職過，在校園環境中總會有個體認，自己有證照和高學歷，如果也寫了好的履歷，就必定能獲取面試公司的青睞，但實情並非如此，事實上許多公司收到很多履歷，求職的畢業生是沒有工作經驗的，這在要說服面試官錄用你還是需要努力的，就像是暢銷書中說的，履歷列表僅是清單，無法打動人，例如在面試中你可能還要在個性上打動對方等等，這也是為什麼同樣的證照和學歷，有的人獲得錄用，而有的人落選。最後提到幸運確實是個影響因素。

Step 2　次個段落中提到了另一本暢銷書《幸運如何發生》，以名公司的總經理說的話為開頭，講述「你必須要擁有幸運才能拿到工作」。接續以《慾望師奶》和《成功的方程式》中的實例，以更有趣的方式陳述出幸運扮演的角色和你也必須替自己創造幸運。

- 這個段落主要提到的是讚美，或許大家都禮貌性的向面試官打招呼然後坐下，你的一些舉動像是讚美，可能就讓你稍微突出些，更不同等等的。

Step 3　下個段落提到了其他特點，當然也都與幸運有關，仍讓人與之共鳴的部分也是影響因素，段落結尾還提到了別說謊，因為會有背景調查等等的。

Step 4　最後以「幸運」是必須的，我們確實需要它的幫助來結尾。

143

經由先前的演練後，現在請看整篇範文並聆聽音檔

Most graduates misconstrue that listing several certificates and having a fancy degree are enough for their job search, but it is just for the first screening. In one of the bestsellers, *The Defining Decade*, it sets interviewees straight. "Resumes are just lists, and lists are not compelling." Those accomplishments listed on the resume only get HR personnel intrigued or meet the major criteria. Interviewees still need to go through the written and several interviews to get the offer. During these processes, anything can happen, and hiring can be more complicated than we imagine. There are multiple factors that will influence how one gets hired, including luck.

許多畢業生誤解了，列出證照和有亮麗的學歷對於他們找工作就足夠了，但是這僅是對於初次篩選。在其中一本暢銷書中，《關鍵十年》，它導正了面試者們的觀念。「履歷僅是清單，而清單一點都不引人注目」。那些列於履歷表上的成就僅能讓人事專員感到有興趣或是達到主要的標準。面試者仍需要經歷

過筆試和幾次的面試才能獲得錄取通知。在這些過程中，任何
事情都可能發生，而雇用比我們想像中更為複雜。有著眾多因
素會影響一個人如何獲得錄取通知，包含幸運。

In *"How Luck Happens"*, the managing director at
Goldman Sachs said that "you are going to need luck to
get a job", and it is true that luck does play a huge role in
whether a person will get the job or not. As we often hear
what others say "create your own luck". Most graduates
just don't know how, doing something is better than doing
nothing. In Desperate Housewives, season 1, Tom
compliments the picture of the boat on the principal's
table, although doing this does not move the principal. (at
least he does something) In *The Success Equation*, the
author accolades the executive's taste in trash cans. Luck
does work in his favor, and later one of the leaders told
him "the six interviewers voted against hiring you", but
"the head guy overrode their assessment and insisted we
bring you in." Of course, there are more than
complimenting things that we can do.

在《幸運如何發生》，高盛公司的總經理說到「你必須要擁有

幸運才能拿到工作」，而這是千真萬確的，幸運確實在一個人能否獲取一份工作中扮演了重大的角色。如同通常我們常聽到其他人說的「創造屬於你自己的幸運」。大多數的畢業生卻不知道要從何下手，做點事比起什麼事都不做好多了。在《慾望師奶》第一季，湯姆讚美了校長桌上的一張船的相片，儘管這個舉動並沒有打動校長（至少他做了些什麼）。在《成功的方程式》，作者讚美高階主管對於垃圾桶的品味。幸運確實站在他那邊，而在稍後，其中一位領導人告訴他「有六位面試官在雇用時對你投下了反對票」，但是「主要決策者的決定壓過了他們的評估並堅持我們要錄用你」。當然，比起讚美事情，我們還有很多事情可以做。

Luck can also be the personality and charm that you exude. Sometimes in a more casual interview, nothing professional is involved. Showing the best side of you or discussing your hobby can sometimes be the click to interviewers. Like, I cannot believe that we went to the same golf club or we both love A team. Sometimes it is related to your childhood. Any bad or sad memory can be the click to someone who is about to make the hiring decision, but do not pretend to be someone who is clearly not yours because often there is a background check that follows right after the interview.

幸運也可以是你所散發出的個性和魅力。有時候在更隨意一些的面試中，沒有任何專業知識牽涉在其中。展現你最好的一面或是討論你的嗜好有時候可以是打動面試官的一擊。像是，我不敢相信我們去同間高爾夫球俱樂部或是我們都同樣喜愛 A 隊伍。有時候與你的童年有關係。任何糟的或傷心的記憶也可以是打動即將要僱用你的人的決定，但是別假裝成顯然不是你本身的人，因為通常在面試後通常都會有背景調查。

To sum up, when it comes to finding a job, resting on a great resume is not enough, and we do need luck to work in our favor. All of us should think outside the box and make it happen.

總之，當提及找工作時，仰賴很棒的履歷是不足夠的，而且我們確實需要幸運站到我們這邊。我們所有人應該要跳脫框架思考並讓它成真。

UNIT 05

唸名校、進入頂尖企業且獲取高薪的工作，這樣的人生規劃，長遠來看是好還是不好呢？

Writing Task 2 ▶ *MP3 023*

TOPIC

In life, people pursue a prestigious degree, get the best internship, and so on in the hope of getting into the top company. Super achievers never fail to impress potential employers and always meet the expectation of their parents and the society. But somehow something goes wrong and they kind of get lost during the process, what do you think the reasons behind this phenomenon? Use specific examples to explain this.

Write at least 250 words

整合能力強化 ❶ 實際演練

請搭配左頁的題目和並構思和完成大作文的演練。

_____

_____

_____

_____

_____

_____

_____

_____

_____

_____

_____

_____

_____

_____

_____

_____

_____

_____

Part 1
雅思寫作 Task1：精選高分字彙

Part 2
雅思寫作 Task1：圖表題小作文

Part 3
雅思寫作 Task2：大作文

整合能力強化 ❷ 單句中譯英演練

　　在掌握文法句型後,學習者大多能拿到 7 分以上的寫作成績,英語句型多樣性是獲取高分的關鍵,現在請演練接下來的單句中譯英練習。請務必演練後再觀看答案,也可以搭配範文音檔強化對各句型的記憶。

❶ 「許多學生太專注於獲取對的分數,這樣他們才能夠進入對的學校,但如此卻使得他們無法從事些不尋常的事」。

_____

_____

【參考答案】

"Many students are so focused on getting the right grades, so they can get into the right school that it barely gives them the chance to try something zany."

❷ 不論是關於獲得分數或是有理想的工作,因此而讓人稱羨,有著非常確定的目標是很棒的,但是有時候執著會帶來的害處多過好處。

_____

_____

【參考答案】

Whether it is about getting grades or having desired jobs that can make people instantly envious, having a very specific goal is great, but sometimes fixation can do more harm than good.

❸ 人們繼續追求他們認為會讓人們忌妒或令人稱羨的事物，但是於
此同時卻也未考慮到他們內在的感受和過程。

_____

_____

【參考答案】

People keep chasing what they deem will make people jealous
and covetous, but at the same time fail to consider their inner
feelings and processes.

❹ 有些畢業生像是超級目標達成者，而從一開始甚至是在他們大一
期間，他們已經視察過所有享譽盛名的公司的所有實習機會，並
做了所有必要的步驟來達到目的。

_____

_____

【參考答案】

Some graduates are like super achievers, and right from the start
or even during their freshman year, they have checked all
internships from prestigious companies and made all the
necessary steps to get there.

❺ 他們獲取卓越的成績並無所不用其極，只要在面試官們的眼中，
這些舉動會得到更額外的分數。

_____

_____

They get excellent grades and do whatever they can as long as it will earn extra points in the eye of the interviewers.

❻ 他們最終達到他們想要的，而且有些甚至上了新聞，聲稱他們對於未來世代是最前程似錦的明日之星，但是在內心深處他們卻感到不快樂。

_____

_____

They eventually get what they want and some even appear in the news as the most promising future stars for the future generation, but clearly, they are unhappy deep down.

❼ 在其他畢業生的眼裡，他們認為辭掉如此棒的工作是多麼白癡的事。在一年之內能夠賺取那樣多的錢是多麼罕見的事。

_____

_____

To the eyes of other graduates, they think what an idiot to quit such a fantastic job. What a rare opportunity to earn such amount of money in a year.

❽ 對於那些前程似錦的星星們，他們認為他們無法再繼續下去了。

【參考答案】

For those promising stars, they think they can no longer do it.

❾ 對於他們來說，這當中似乎有那些地方出了差錯了？在《第一份
工作》，克瑞格・山道士坦承「我花費了數年達到目標，但是我
並未真的替自己決定過此事」。

【參考答案】

In *First Jobs*, Craig Dos Santos admits "I had spent years to get there, but I didn't really ever decide this."

❿ 忽略那些津貼、股票選擇和金錢，傾聽你的心是最棒的做法。

【參考答案】

Neglecting those benefits, stock options, and money and listening to you heart are the best thing to do.

TOPIC

In life, people pursue a prestigious degree, get the best internship, and so on in the hope of getting into the top company. Super achievers never fail to impress potential employers and always meet the expectation of their parents and the society. But somehow something goes wrong and they kind of get lost during the process, what do you think the reasons behind this phenomenon? Use specific examples to explain this.

搭配的暢銷書

- *Getting There*《勝利，並非事事順利：30 位典範人物不藏私的人生真心話》
- *First Jobs*《第一份工作》

Step 1 題目是關於不斷替自己設定目標的 super achiever，但是隨著目標逐漸達成，例如上名校、進入知名公司工作等，這些人並不快樂。他們確實達到了父母和社會的期待，也成了新聞中的明日之星，文中要探討的是，當中到底出了哪些問題呢？首段以暢銷書《勝利，並非事事順利：30 位典

範人物不藏私的人生真心話》破題，太專注於做某些事情時，導致你過於侷限，且並未自我充分探索，最終過了數年後目標達成了，才發現自己當初並未好好思考過這些適不適合自己。

Step 2　次個段落進一步描述到，只要是能在面試官面前有所加分的事情，他們都會盡其所能的去做，也指出達到目標後他們的不快樂，而周遭人更無法理解他們辭掉工作的原因。（因為他們像是人生勝利組賺取許多金錢。）

Step 3　末段以另一本暢銷書《第一份工作》點出問題所在，其實作者最終意識到自己並未替自己做決定過，只是不斷達成目標。文章後續接著推論出要傾聽自己內心聲音並從事自己真的想要做的事情，最後以如此才不會有所遺憾，並享受自己應獲得的快樂。

經由先前的演練後，現在請看整篇範文並聆聽音檔

In *Getting There*, Stacey Snider shares her wisdom about making a decision. "Many students are so focused on getting the right grades, so they can get into the right school that it barely gives them the chance to try something zany." Whether it is about getting grades or having desired jobs that can make people instantly envious, having a very specific goal is great, but sometimes fixation can do more harm than good. People keep chasing what they deem will make people jealous and covetous, but at the same time fail to consider their inner feelings and processes.

在《勝利，並非事事順利：30 位典範人物不藏私的人生真心話》一書中，史黛西・史奈德分享了關於她做決定的智慧。「許多學生太專注於獲取對的分數，這樣他們才能夠進入對的學校，但如此卻使得他們無法從事些不尋常的事」。不論是關於獲得分數或是有理想的工作，因此而讓人稱羨，有著非常確定的目標是很棒的，但是有時候執著會帶來的害處多過好處。

人們繼續追求他們認為會讓人們忌妒或令人稱羨的事物，但是
與此同時卻也未考慮到他們內在的感受和過程。

Some graduates are like super achievers, and right from
the start or even during their freshman year, they have
checked all internships from prestigious companies and
made all the necessary steps to get there. They get
excellent grades and do whatever they can as long as it
will earn extra points in the eyes of the interviewers. They
eventually get what they want and some even appear in
the news as the most promising future stars for the future
generation, but clearly, they are unhappy deep down. To
the eyes of other graduates, they think what an idiot to
quit such a fantastic job. What a rare opportunity to earn
such amount of money in a year. For those promising
stars, they think they can no longer do it.

有些畢業生像是超級目標達成者，而從一開始甚至是在他們大
一期間，他們已經視察過所有享譽盛名的公司的所有實習機
會，並做了所有必要的步驟來達到目的。他們獲取卓越的成績
並無所不用其極，只要在面試官們的眼中，這些舉動會得到更
額外的分數。他們最終達到他們想要的，而且有些甚至上了新

聞，聲稱他們對於未來世代是最前程似錦的明日之星，但是在內心深處，他們卻感到不快樂。在其他畢業生的眼裡，他們認為辭掉如此棒的工作是多麼白癡的事。在一年之內能夠賺取那樣多的錢是多麼罕見的事。對於那些前程似錦的明日之星們，他們認為他們無法再繼續下去了。

What seems to go wrong for them? In *First Jobs*, Craig Dos Santos admits "I had spent years to get there, but I didn't really ever decide this." This is the answer and you have to have the work experience to know what it means. If you really explore and figure what you truly want, then you won't even apply for an internship in the first place. Doing what others deem important or successful is what engulfs the mind of the future generations, and it won't last long. You have to really decide the career path for yourself. If you do not want to be a software engineer, then why do you go after the company internship and then possibly the interview later. Pleasing people around you, such as parents and professors or meeting the norm of the social standard is wrong. Neglecting those benefits, stock options, and money and listening to you heart are the best thing to do. With the right mindset, you won't regret doing those things, and have the happiness you deserve.

對於他們來說，這當中似乎有哪些地方出了差錯了？在《第一份工作》，克瑞格·山道士坦承「我花費了數年達到目標，但是我並未真的替自己決定過此事」。這就是答案，而你必須要有工作經驗去知道這意謂著什麼。如果你真的探索且了解到你真的想要什麼，那麼你甚至就不會在起初去申請實習機會。做著其他人認為重要或成功的事情吞噬掉未來世代的心智，而且這持續不久。你必須要替自己的職涯真正做下決定。如果你不想要成為軟體工程師，那麼你為什麼參加了公司的實習以及可能於稍後的面試。討好你周遭的人，例如父母和教授或是達到社會標準的規範是錯誤的。忽略那些津貼、股票選擇和金錢，傾聽你的心是最棒的做法。有著對的心態，你不會遺憾去做那些事情，而且能享有你所值得的快樂。

UNIT 06

工作中常會遇到的問題，「金錢」和「夢想」只能二選一，你又會如何抉擇呢？

 Writing Task 2 ▶ *MP3 025*

TOPIC

In life, there are multiple dilemmas, and one of the biggest is choosing between money and dream. Some choose a job that offers a much higher salary, while others pick the job they love, but come with price of getting minimum wages. Sometimes reality is so cruel that it keeps multiple graduates from pursuing their dreams. Do you think people should pursue their dreams or should they pursue money? Use specific examples and explain.

Write at least 250 words

整合能力強化 ❶ 實際演練

請搭配左頁的題目和並構思和完成大作文的演練。

_____

_____

_____

_____

_____

_____

_____

_____

_____

_____

_____

_____

_____

_____

_____

_____

_____

_____

_____

在掌握文法句型後，學習者大多能拿到 7 分以上的寫作成績，英語句型多樣性是獲取高分的關鍵，現在請演練接下來的單句中譯英練習。請務必演練後再觀看答案，也可以搭配範文音檔強化對各句型的記憶。

❶ 大多數畢業生對於他們是否該選擇較高薪的工作，還是該追求他們理想的工作，但卻僅能提供他們微薄薪資有著進退兩難的困境。

_____

_____

【參考答案】

Most graduates have the dilemma of whether they should choose a job that has a much higher salary or whether they should pursue their ideal job that only gives them meager paycheck.

❷ 這是對於許多 20 多歲的人的困境，他們不具工作經驗或僅有些許工作經驗。

_____

_____

【參考答案】

It is the predicament for many twentysomethings who have zero work experiences or have little work experiences.

❸ 也千真萬確的是，他們大多數的人大學畢業後，從事著與他們本科系全然無關的工作。

_____

_____

【參考答案】

It is also true that most of them graduating out of the university doing jobs totally unrelated to their majors.

❹ 有些最終獲取工作成了房地產經紀人賺取大把鈔票。即使他們有些人賺取比他們同儕更多的金錢，像是這樣的問題縈繞在他們心中，尤其是當他們獨自一人時。

_____

_____

【參考答案】

Some eventually get the job as realtors earning lots of money. Even if some of them are earning more money than their peers, questions like these linger in their minds, especially when they are alone.

❺ 其他人賺取了很多錢，但是最終辭掉了他們的工作，追求他們真正所愛的工作。

_____

_____

【參考答案】

Others are earning lots of money, but eventually quit their jobs by pursuing what they truly love.

❻ 當然，對於此決定沒有所謂的對或錯的答案。人們對於台幣賺取超過一百萬者的評論大不相同。

_____

_____

【參考答案】
Of course, there are no right or wrong answers to this. Comments about people earning more a million NT dollars a year vary.

❼ 有的人替他們辯護，藉由述說著他們做對的事情。有些工作確實需要你做幾個轉換而且有相當重的工作量。

_____

_____

【參考答案】
Some say they are insane because they quit their jobs. Others defend them by saying that they are doing the right thing. Some jobs do require you to make several shifts and have a heavy workload.

❽ 最後，這確實對於他們的健康造成了很大的傷害。既然健康比起財富來說更為重要，他們之所以辭掉工作也是合理的。還有其他人辭掉工作是因為他們對於他們所從事的工作並沒有感到熱情。

_____

_____

【參考答案】

Eventually, it does take a toll on their health. Since health is above wealth, they are reasonable enough to quit. Still others quit the jobs because they are not passionate about what they are doing.

❾ 這像是在浪費他們的生命。對於所從事的工作不是你所熱愛的是很難維持下去的。在《你如何衡量你的人生》，它述說到「唯一使你真的感到滿足是從事你認為是偉大的工作，而唯一能做出驚人之作是要喜愛你所從事的。」

_____

_____

【參考答案】

It's like they are wasting their life. It is hard to sustain the effort doing things that are not what you love. In *How Will You Measure Your Life*, it states the fact that "The only way to be truly satisfied is to do what you believe is great work. And the only way to do great work is to love what you do."

❿ 賈伯斯確實預見了 20 幾歲的人和 30 幾歲的人所遭遇到的進退兩難的困境。

_____

_____

【參考答案】

Steve Jobs certainly foresees the dilemma that twentysomethings and thirtysomethings encounter.

TOPIC

In life, there are multiple dilemmas, and one of the biggest is choosing between money and dream. Some choose a job that offers a much higher salary, while others pick the job they love, but come with price of getting minimum wages. Sometimes reality is so cruel that it keeps multiple graduates from pursuing their dreams. Do you think people should pursue their dreams or should they pursue money? Use specific examples and explain.

搭配的暢銷書

- *How Will You Measure Your Life*《你如何衡量你的人生》
- *Where You Go Is Not Who You Will Be*《你所讀的學校並非你能成為什麼樣的人》

Step 1 這題提到了關於理想和金錢的選擇。先定義了大學畢業生的困境（追求理想等同要放棄許多，甚至獲取更低的薪資，影響生活品質等），緊接著提到了從事與本科系無關的工作。例子中提到了從事房地產經紀人賺取大把鈔票，但終究不長久，有許多人後來還是辭掉這些高薪工作。

166

Step 2 次段提到了幾個論述，並推論出「還有其他人辭掉工作是因為他們對於他們所從事的工作並沒有感到熱情。」這是一個關鍵點。進一步以暢銷書《你如何衡量你的人生》的論點點出這是 20 幾歲的人和 30 幾歲的人所遭遇到的進退兩難的困境。

Step 3 末段提到了，金錢的流逝速度。並以暢銷書《你所讀的學校並非你能成為什麼樣的人》，它說到「你將會了解到如何賺錢，一旦你了解自己所愛的是什麼」。它提到了很重要的論點。最後以「擇你所愛」並對你來說是有價值的才是更重要的。

Part 1
雅思寫作 Task1：精選高分字彙

Part 2
雅思寫作 Task1：圖表題小作文

Part 3
雅思寫作 Task2：大作文

167

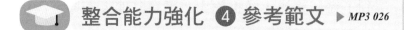

經由先前的演練後，現在請看整篇範文並聆聽音檔

Most graduates have the dilemma of whether they should choose a job that has a much higher salary or whether they should pursue their ideal job that only gives them meager paycheck. It is the predicament for many twentysomethings who have zero work experiences or have little work experiences. It is also true that most of them graduating out of the university doing jobs totally unrelated to their majors. Some eventually get the job as realtors earning lots of money. Even if some of them are earning more money than their peers, questions like these linger in their minds, especially when they are alone. Others are earning lots of money, but eventually quit their jobs by pursuing what they truly love.

大多數畢業生對於他們是否該選擇較高薪的工作，還是該追求他們理想的工作，但卻僅能提供他們微薄薪資有著進退兩難的困境。這是對於許多 20 多歲的人的困境，他們不具工作經驗或僅有些許工作經驗。也千真萬確的是，他們大多數的人大學畢業後，從事著與他們本科系全然無關的工作。有些最終獲取工作成了房地產經紀人賺取大把鈔票。即使他們有些人賺取比他們同儕更多的金錢，像是這樣的問題縈繞在他們心中，尤其是當他們獨自一人時。其他人賺取了很多錢，但是最終辭掉了他們的工作，追求他們真正所愛的工作。

Of course, there are no right or wrong answers to this. Comments about people earning more a million NT dollars a year vary. Some say they are insane because they quit their jobs. Others defend them by saying that they are doing the right thing. Some jobs do require you to make several shifts and have a heavy workload. Eventually, it does take a toll on their health. Since health is above wealth, they are reasonable enough to quit. Still others quit the jobs because they are not passionate about what they are doing. It's like they are wasting their life. It is hard to sustain the effort doing things that are not what you love. In *How Will You Measure Your Life*, it states the fact that "The only way to be truly satisfied is to do what you believe is great work. And the only way to do great work is to love what you do." Steve Jobs certainly foresees the dilemma that twentysomethings and thirtysomethings encounter.

當然，對於此決定沒有所謂的對或錯的答案。人們對於台幣賺取超過一百萬者的評論大不相同。有的人替他們辯護，藉由述說著他們是做對的事情。有些工作確實需要你做幾個轉換而且有相當重的工作量。最後，這確實對於他們的健康造成了很大的傷害。既然健康比起財富來說更為重要，他們之所以辭掉工作也是合理的。還有其他人辭掉工作是因為他們對於他們所從事的工作並沒有感到熱情。這像是在浪費他們的生命。對於所從事的工作不是你所熱愛的是很難維持下去的。在《你如何衡量你的人生》，它述說到「唯一使你真的感到滿足是從事你認為是偉大的工作，而唯一能做出驚人之作是要喜愛你所從事的。」賈伯斯確實預見了 20 幾歲的人和 30 幾歲的人所遭遇到的進退兩難的困境。

Furthermore, money comes and goes very quickly. It is true that those realtors make a lot of money in a few years, but they also lose it in a quick fashion. In *Where You Go Is Not Who You Will Be*, it says "you'll figure out how to make money once you figure out what you love to do." People who choose to do what they truly love by quitting the job of a million NT dollars later are more successful than before. To sum up, we should really focus on the long-term rather on the short-term. High salaries may give us an immediate benefit, but life is long. Doing what you love and what really has values to you is more important.

此外，金錢來的快去得也快。千真萬確的是，那些房地產經理人在幾年內賺取了許多錢，但是他們也以很快的方式流失掉金錢。在《你所讀的學校並非你能成為什麼樣的人》，它說到「你將會了解到如何賺錢，一旦你了解自己所愛的是什麼」。人們選擇了他們真的所愛的事情，進而辭掉了百萬年薪的工作，最終卻比先前更加成功。總之，我們應該要將重心放長遠，而非短期上。高薪可能給予我們立即的益處，但是人生是長久的。擇你所愛並對你來說是有價值的才是更重要的。

Part 1
雅思寫作 Task1：精選高分字彙

Part 2
雅思寫作 Task1：圖表題小作文

Part 3
雅思寫作 Task2：大作文

UNIT 07

如何知道選擇的工作是否適合自己呢？如何能夠避免自己的人生「黃金時段」花費在不適合的公司呢？

Writing Task 2 ▶ MP3 027

TOPIC

As a saying goes, five years after you graduate determine most of your adult life, and it is true that if you don't succeed in the timeframe, it is very unlikely for you to achieve something great in your later life. If your golden years are so important, the company you choose to work for matters, and how does one avoid getting deceived by the company which cannot make you a more successful person. Use specific examples and explain.

Write at least 250 words

整合能力強化 ❶ 實際演練

請搭配左頁的題目和並構思和完成大作文的演練。

_____

_____

_____

_____

_____

_____

_____

_____

_____

_____

_____

_____

_____

_____

_____

_____

　　在掌握文法句型後，學習者大多能拿到 7 分以上的寫作成績，英語句型多樣性是獲取高分的關鍵，現在請演練接下來的單句中譯英練習。請務必演練後再觀看答案，也可以搭配範文音檔強化對各句型的記憶。

❶ 幾乎每個人都知道畢業後的那年，大多可能是 24 或 25 歲到 10 年後是人生中的黃金時期。有些人將其稱為人生中的黃金時段。

_____

_____

【參考答案】

Almost everyone knows the year after they graduate, most likely 24 or 25 to ten years later is the golden year of the lifetime. Some call it the prime time of the life.

❷ 其他人，即使他們知道他們應該要珍惜這個時段，不管怎樣仍將其揮霍掉了。

_____

_____

【參考答案】

Others, even if they know they should cherish the time, still squander it away.

❸ 專家和學者們都告誡年輕世代要把握黃金時段，存錢等等的，這樣一來他們就不會到了 30 幾歲或是 40 幾歲時，回頭看後有很多的遺憾在。

_____

_____

【參考答案】

Experts and scholars all caution younger generations about seizing the prime time, saving money, and so on, so that they won't look back and have lots of regrets in their thirties or forties.

❹ 還有其他人已經聽了那些的專家講述的，而開始了真的節約的生活型態等等的。

_____

_____

【參考答案】

Still others have listened to what those experts have said and start a really frugal style and so on.

❺ 他們都想要有很棒的工作而且有成功的職涯，但是他們卻不得其所。

_____

_____

【參考答案】

They all want to have a great job and have a successful career, but they just don't know how.

❻ 他們不具有許多工作經驗，所以這使得他們像是餐桌上待宰的羔羊。

_____

_____

【參考答案】

They do not have many work experiences so this makes them the lamb on the dinner plate.

❼ 他們不需要對一些問題做出回應，而且詢問他們的同儕和朋友似乎只有些許或全然無任何助益。

_____

_____

【參考答案】

They don't have to respond to some questions and asking their peers and friends seem to be of little or no help.

❽ 他們如何知道他們所工作的公司對於他們來說是理想的或是他們如何得知這時間是花到刀口上呢？既然時間真的飛逝而且你沒有時光機讓你能回頭再來。

_____

_____

【參考答案】

How do they know the company they are working for is ideal for them or how do they know it's the time well-spent? Since time really flies and you don't have the time machine for you to go back.

❾ 女主角有某種感覺，就是「它們公司的領導者欺騙式地籠絡她，占用她黃金時段時的時間和天賦」。

_____

_____

【參考答案】

The heroine has the feelings that "its leaders had deceptively co-opted her time and talents in the prime of her life."

❿ 你必須要知道，即使公司沒有錢付下個月的薪資或是即將破產，老闆總是會守口如瓶，只有他或她自己知道這回事。

_____

_____

【參考答案】

You have to know even if the company has no money to pay next month's salary or is about to go bankrupt, the boss always keeps this to himself or herself.

TOPIC

As a saying goes, five years after you graduate determine most of your adult life, and it is true that if you don't succeed in the timeframe, it is very unlikely for you to achieve something great in your later life. If your golden years are so important, the company you choose to work for matters, and how does one avoid getting deceived by the company which cannot make you a more successful person. Use specific examples and explain.

搭配的暢銷書

■ *How Will You Measure Your Life*《你如何衡量你的人生》

Step 1　首段先定義黃金時段，黃金時段確實對年輕人後期生活有很重大的影響，並告誡這樣在到了某個年紀時，才能不會有遺憾，並提到確實有些人照著專家的建議開始過節約生活。

Step 2　次段提到年輕世代關心的還是工作，而不具工作經驗讓他們很吃虧。緊接著進一步講述到，因為這段時期的重要性，所以替哪間公司工作很重要，因為這段時間是無法重

頭的。

Step 3　下個段落提到暢銷書《你如何衡量你的人生》，從案例中可以得知女主角的黃金時段被一間公司騙了，公司給了假的承諾，接著進行論述，提到一些關於職場的想法。最後提到暢銷書中的解決辦法。其實大學時的實習機會就是一個可以多認識這間公司的管道，比起畢業後求職，然後簽約或在某間公司上班後，才開始認識公司，更能掌握這家公司的發展方向適不適合自己，最後總結出，此能大幅降低被騙的機會。

Part 1
雅思寫作 Task1 : 精選高分字彙

Part 2
雅思寫作 Task1 : 圖表題 小作文

Part 3
雅思寫作 Task2 : 大作文

經由先前的演練後，現在請看整篇範文並聆聽音檔

Almost everyone knows the year after they graduate, most likely 24 or 25 to ten years later is the golden year of the lifetime. Some call it the prime time of the life. Others, even if they know they should cherish the time, still squander it away. Experts and scholars all caution younger generations about seizing the prime time, saving money, and so on, so that they won't look back and have lots of regrets in their thirties or forties. Still others have listened to what those experts have said and start a really frugal style and so on.

幾乎每個人都知道畢業後的那年，大多可能是 24 或 25 歲到 10 年後是人生中的黃金時期。有些人將其稱為人生中的黃金時段。其他人，即使他們知道他們應該要珍惜這個時段，不管怎樣仍將其揮霍掉了。專家和學者們都告誡年輕世代要把握黃金時段，存錢等等的，這樣一來他們就不會到了 30 幾歲或是 40 幾歲時，回頭看後有很多的遺憾在。還有其他人已經聽了那些的專家講述的而開始了真的節約的生活型態等等的。

What puzzles most younger generations is still related to the jobs. They all want to have a great job and have a successful career, but they just don't know how. They do not have many work experiences so this makes them the lamb on the dinner plate. They don't have to respond to some questions and asking their peers and friends seem to be of little or no help. How do they know the company they are working for is ideal for them or how do they know it's the time well-spent? Since time really flies and you don't have the time machine for you to go back.

而困惑大多數年輕世代的仍與工作有關連。他們都想要有很棒的工作而且有成功的職涯，但是他們卻不得其所。他們不具有許多工作經驗，所以這使得他們像是餐桌上待宰的羔羊。他們不需要對一些問題做出回應，而且詢問他們的同儕和朋友似乎只有些許或全然無任何助益。他們如何知道他們所工作的公司對於他們來說是理想的或是他們如何得知這時間是花到刀口上呢？既然時間真的飛逝而且你沒有時光機讓你能回頭再來。

In *How Will You Measure Your Life*, it discusses a case that is related to this problem. The heroine has the feelings that "its leaders had deceptively co-opted her time and talents in the prime of her life." Bosses and leaders all have a way of saying that deceives or fools you into believing that working in their companies is the best decision that you have ever made. You have to know even if the company has no money to pay next month's salary or is about to go bankrupt, the boss always keeps this to himself or herself. You do not have to trust everything the boss tells you, and you do not have to go paranoid about things you have heard. In the book, the author offers a solution to this problem. "Perhaps she could have opted for an internship before committing to a full-time job." It's one of the solutions. Observations are the key. During the time of being an intern there, you have the time to examine whether the company is going in the right path and so on. Those observations can significantly minimize the chance of getting deceived.

在《你如何衡量你的人生》，它討論了關於這個問題的一則案例。女主角有某種感覺，就是「她們公司的領導者欺騙式地籠絡她，占用她黃金時段的時間和天賦」。老闆們和領導著們都有這樣的一套說法，欺騙或愚弄你，讓你誤信替他們的公司工作是你所做過的最佳決定。你必須要知道，即使公司沒有錢付下個月的薪資或是即將破產，老闆總是會守口如瓶，只有他或她自己知道這回事。你沒有必要去相信你的老闆所告訴你的每件事，你也不用對於你所聽到的事感到偏執。在書中，作者提供了對於這個問題的解決之道。「或許她可以在向公司承諾全職工作前，先實習看看」。這是其中一個解決之道。觀察是個關鍵。在那裡擔任實習生的期間，你有時間去檢視一間公司是否走在對的道路上等等的。那些觀察可能很大程度地減低被騙的機會。

UNIT 08

工作中也會面臨在「累積經驗」和「獲取更多金錢」的抉擇，如果同時錄取兩間都是不錯的公司，又該如何選擇呢？

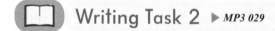

Writing Task 2 ▶ MP3 029

TOPIC

Although it is quite unlikely to happen in real life, it does happen sometimes. And what if you get both fantastic offers, one actually gives you an exceedingly high salary, while another can offer you the chance to grow but with a much lower salary. What decision will you make? Choosing money over experience or picking experience over money. Use specific examples and explain.

Write at least 250 words

🎓 整合能力強化 ❶ 實際演練

請搭配左頁的題目和並構思和完成大作文的演練。

_____

_____

_____

_____

_____

_____

_____

_____

_____

_____

_____

_____

_____

_____

整合能力強化 ❷ 單句中譯英演練

在掌握文法句型後，學習者大多能拿到 7 分以上的寫作成績，英語句型多樣性是獲取高分的關鍵，現在請演練接下來的單句中譯英練習。請務必演練後再觀看答案，也可以搭配範文音檔強化對各句型的記憶。

❶ 獲取兩份很棒的工作錄取通知對於求職候選人來說絕對是很大的喜悅，但是知道如何選擇哪份工作更適合自己是數百萬的畢業生所面臨的困境。

_____

_____

【參考答案】

Getting two fantastic job offers is absolutely a great joy for the job candidates, but knowing how to choose which one is more suitable for you is the dilemma for millions of graduates.

❷ 如果 A 公司提供的金錢遠高於 B 公司，而 B 公司卻能滋養你，提供你所需要的經驗，你也能於接下來的 10 年茁壯成長，那麼你會如何做出選擇呢？

_____

_____

【參考答案】

If company A offers significantly more money than company B, whereas company B can nourish you with the experience necessary for you to be robust enough for the next 10 years, then what would you choose.

❸ 那麼，這已經成了在經驗和金錢中做出選擇的問題了。

_____

_____

【參考答案】

Then it has become the question of choosing between experience and money.

❹ 甚至多 5000 元台幣對大學畢業生來說很多，因為這意謂著一年多了六萬元的收入，你不需要是擅長於數學的專家去了解這點。

_____

_____

【參考答案】

Even earning NT 5,000 dollars more will mean so much for university graduates because that's 60,000 dollars more in a year, and you don't have to be an expert who is good at math to realize it.

❺ 有些人說當機會敲門時，你必須要抓住且在你 30 歲前累積最多的金錢。

_____

_____

【參考答案】

Some say that when opportunities knock on the door, you have got to grasp and accumulate the most money before you turn thirty.

❻ 其他人則是勸阻你別僅僅追求金錢，反而鼓勵你去珍惜經驗，這樣一來你就不會於稍後有所遺憾，而兩方的立場也都有些令人信服的點存在。

_____

_____

【參考答案】

Others discourage you from pursuing solely for money and encourage you to value the experience so that you won't regret later, and both parties have some valid points.

❼ 而 Lehman Brothers 在當時很龐大，而且它能夠提供相當高的薪資。其中一位作者的人生指導員，喬治・史丹登提供了他的洞察。

_____

_____

【參考答案】

And Lehman Brothers was huge at that time and it can offer considerably higher pay. One of the author's mentors, George Stanton offers his insight.

❽ 「在人生中，確實會有時期是你應該要選擇金錢大於經驗」，「但是做那樣的選擇時，是當利潤是更大時，當利潤是數百萬美元，而不是數千元」。這確實是個引導我們思考為什麼的好方

式。

_____

_____

【參考答案】

"There actually will be times in life when you should choose money over experience", "but make that choice when the margin is much bigger, when the margin is millions of dollars, not thousand." It is actually a good way to lead us to think about why.

❾ 長遠來看，經驗比金錢還重要，而且當利潤很少時，你應該要選擇經驗。在找工作期間或轉職時，經驗法則總是一樣的。

_____

_____

【參考答案】

For the long term, experience is more important than money, and when the margin is very little, you should choose experience. During the job search or job hop, the rule is always the same.

❿ 你不會因為另一間公司提供你高於現在公司給的薪資兩千元就決定要跳槽到另一間公司。

_____

_____

【參考答案】

You do not make a job hop just because another company offers you NT 2,000 more dollars than the salary that the current company offers you.

189

Part 1　雅思寫作 Task1：精選高分字彙

Part 2　雅思寫作 Task1：圖表題小作文

Part 3　雅思寫作 Task2：大作文

TOPIC

Although it is quite unlikely to happen in real life, it does happen sometimes. And what if you get both fantastic offers, one actually gives you an exceedingly high salary, while another can offer you the chance to grow but with a much lower salary. What decision will you make? Choosing money over experience or picking experience over money. Use specific examples and explain.

搭配的暢銷書

- "*The Promise of the Pencil* : how an ordinary person can create an extraordinary change" 《一支鉛筆的承諾：一位普通人如何能創造出驚人的改變》

Step 1　題目詢問到如果同時接獲兩個極佳的錄取通知時，該選擇什麼呢？這題是詢問在金錢和經驗中做出選擇，而太模糊或不具體的表達其實等同沒有表達且更難獲取 7 以上的成績。首段先定義，並以詼諧的字句結尾，「...因為這意謂著一年多了六萬元的收入，你不需要是位擅長數學的專家去了解這點。」，但這也並不表明會選擇金錢的立場。

Step 2　　次段很簡潔且流暢表明出兩方立場，論點看似都很令人信服。

Step 3　　下一段以暢銷書《一支鉛筆的承諾：一位普通人如何能創造出驚人的改變》中的實例來講述提升說服力，作者的 mentor 喬丹提出的論點很棒，也很能引導我們去思考，因為經驗最終助益最大。

■　（範文中沒提到的是，作者最後選擇 Bain 而非 Lehman Brothers，更令人難置信的是 Lehman Brothers 這樣的大公司後來破產了，作者不禁思考如果選擇該公司自己命運又會是如何呢？而當時他有些朋友也因此面臨長期失業，作者慶幸自己選擇了 Bain）

Step 4　　末段提到，從長遠來看，經驗比金錢還重要，最後講述自己的立場，經由這些推論跟實例後，自己會選擇經驗而非金錢。

經由先前的演練後,現在請看整篇範文並聆聽音檔

Of course, lots of us have doubts that this can't be happening, but in life you just never know because anything can happen. Getting two fantastic job offers is absolutely a great joy for the job candidates, but knowing how to choose which one is more suitable for you is the dilemma for millions of graduates. If company A offers significantly more money than company B, whereas company B can nourish you with the experience necessary for you to be robust enough for the next 10 years, then what would you choose. Then it has become the question of choosing between experience and money. Even earning NT 5,000 dollars more will mean so much for university graduates because that's 60,000 dollars more in a year, and you don't have to be an expert who is good at math to realize it.

當然,我們許多人對此抱持著存疑的態度,這不可能發生,但是在生命中,你永遠無法得知,因為任何事都有可能發生。獲取兩份很棒的工作錄取通知對於求職候選人來說絕對是很大的喜悅，但是知道如何選擇哪份工作更適合自己是數百萬的畢業生所面臨的困境。如果 A 公司提供的金錢遠高於 B 公司，而 B 公司卻能滋養你，提供你所需要的經驗，你也能於接下來的 10 年茁壯成長，那麼你會如何做出選擇呢？那麼，這已經成了在經驗和金錢中做出選擇的問題了。甚至多 5000 元台幣對大學畢業生來說很多，因為這意謂著一年多了六萬元的收入，你不需要是位擅長數學的專家去了解這點。

The debate can go on and on. Some say that when opportunities knock on the door, you have got to grasp and accumulate the most money before you turn thirty. Others discourage you from pursuing solely for money and encourage you to value the experience so that you won't regret later, and both parties have some valid points.

辯論可以不斷持續著。有些人說當機會敲門時，你必須要抓住且在你 30 歲前累積最多的金錢。其他人則是勸阻你別僅僅追求金錢，反而鼓勵你去珍惜經驗，這樣一來你就不會於稍後有所遺憾，而兩方的立場也都有些令人信服的點存在。

In "*The Promise of the Pencil* : how an ordinary person can create an extraordinary change" the author actually faces the predicament like this. Should he choose Bain or Lehman? And Lehman Brothers was huge at that time and it can offer considerably higher pay. One of the author's mentors, George Stanton offers his insight. "There actually will be times in life when you should choose money over experience", "but make that choice when the margin is much bigger, when the margin is millions of dollars, not thousand." It is actually a good way to lead us to think about why.

在《一支鉛筆的承諾：一位普通人如何能創造出驚人的改變》，作者實際上面臨了像是這樣的困境。他應該要選擇 Bain 還是 Lehman 呢？而 Lehman Brothers 在當時很龐大，而且它能夠提供相當高的薪資。其中一位作者的人生導師，喬治・史丹登提供了他的洞察。「在人生中，確實會有時期是你應該要選擇金錢大於經驗」，「但是做那樣的選擇時，是當利潤是更大時，當利潤是數百萬美元，而不是數千元」。這確實是個引導我們思考為什麼的好方式。

For the long term, experience is more important than

money, and when the margin is very little, you should choose experience. During the job search or job hop, the rule is always the same. You do not make a job hop just because another company offers you NT 2,000 dollars more than the salary that the current company offers you. The margin is too little. Instead, you stay in the current company, and after 3-5 years your experience is significantly more valuable, you make a job hop to another company and probably the managerial position. You earn more than that. To sum up, from the above mentioned descriptions, I would choose experience over money.

長遠來看，經驗比金錢還重要，而且當利潤很少時，你應該要選擇經驗。在找工作期間或轉職時，經驗法則總是一樣的。你不會因為另一間公司提供你高於現在公司給的薪資兩千元就決定要跳槽到另一間公司。利潤太些微了。取而代之的是，你應該要待在現在的公司，而在 3 至 5 年後，你的經驗具更多價值時，你跳槽到另一間公司，而這可能是管理職的職缺。你能夠賺取多於那金額的錢。總之，從上述的描述，我會選擇經驗大於金錢。

UNIT 09

想把事情做好是件好事，但是否該對自己過於嚴苛，甚至跟資深同事等相比較呢？有著完美主義的思維對於新鮮人工作的影響又會是什麼呢？

 Writing Task 2 ▶ *MP3 031*

TOPIC

Some graduates set such a high standard for themselves during their first few jobs. They want to perform tasks as good as senior colleagues. The perfectionist mindset actually does them more harm than good, even if the intention is good. Do you think graduates should be so hard on themselves? Use specific examples and explain.

Write at least 250 words

整合能力強化 ❶ 實際演練

請搭配左頁的題目和並構思和完成大作文的演練。

_____

_____

_____

_____

_____

_____

_____

_____

_____

_____

_____

_____

_____

_____

_____

整合能力強化 ❷ 單句中譯英演練

在掌握文法句型後，學習者大多能拿到 7 分以上的寫作成績，英語句型多樣性是獲取高分的關鍵，現在請演練接下來的單句中譯英練習。請務必演練後再觀看答案，也可以搭配範文音檔強化對各句型的記憶。

❶ 大多數的大學畢業生在四年的大學學習期間就做了許多的準備，希望有朝一日能夠進入享譽盛名的公司工作，而且賺取高額的薪資。

_____

_____

【參考答案】

Most university graduates are making lots of preparation during four years of their undergraduate study in the hope of getting in the prestigious company and earning a significantly high salary.

❷ 追求這樣的目標並沒有錯，但是有些卻使得他們本身的健康和職涯遭受相當大的損害。

_____

_____

【參考答案】

There is nothing wrong with the pursuit, but some are making it to be quite damaging to their health and career.

❸ 大學畢業生才剛開始做他們第一份工作，而不知怎麼的，他們對自己要求很嚴苛。

_____

_____

【參考答案】

University graduates are just doing their first job and somehow, they are so hard on themselves.

❹ 有這樣的動機總是好的，因為他們想要做那些能夠驚艷客戶或他們雇主的事情，但是他們還僅是初學者。他們才剛開始學習事物。

_____

_____

【參考答案】

The incentive is always good because they want to do things that can wow the client or their employer, but they are just the beginner. They are just starting to learn things.

❺ 在《關鍵性十年》，丹尼爾的例子闡明了這樣的現象，而實際上更糟。

_____

_____

【參考答案】

In *The Defining Decade*, the case of Danielle illustrates this phenomenon, and actually it is worse.

199

❻ 「事實上，大多數她與之相比較的人，都比她更年長或是在這個行業工作遠比她長久」。這引起了對自己本身太嚴苛的議題。

_____

_____

【參考答案】

"In fact, most of the people she compared herself to were older than she was or had been working longer than she had." This has aroused the issue of being too hard on yourself.

❼ 此舉對於一個人的健康有相當程度的傷害。女主角丹尼爾甚至將她自己與具經驗的同事比較。

_____

_____

【參考答案】

It can harm one's health for quite a bit. The heroine Danielle even compares herself to experienced colleagues.

❽ 你想要向有經驗且把份內工作都做好的同事看齊是件好事，但與此同時，你需要調適自我，因為他們在做那些任務時已經有了幾年的工作經驗了。

_____

_____

【參考答案】

It is good that you want to look up to experienced co-workers who do the job well, but at the same time you need to adjust yourself that they have had a few years of experience in doing those tasks.

❾ 你能夠逐漸交出像那些同事同樣品質的作品，但是你不需要設定太過高的標準，像是你要在幾天內就追趕上他們。

_____

_____

【參考答案】

You can gradually deliver the quality of the work very much the same as theirs, but you do not have to set a too high standard that you want to do that in just a few days.

❿ 過於具有野心可能也會影響你做那份工作的能力。而有些例子，新聘人員辭掉工作因為他們認為自己遠落後於他們的同事。

_____

_____

【參考答案】

Being overly ambitious can ruin your ability to do the work. In some instances, newly recruits quit the job because they think they are lagging behind their co-workers.

TOPIC

Some graduates set such a high standard for themselves during their first few jobs. They want to perform tasks as good as senior colleagues. The perfectionist mindset actually does them more harm than good, even if the intention is good. Do you think graduates should be so hard on themselves? Use specific examples and explain.

搭配的暢銷書

- *The Defining Decade*《關鍵性十年》
- *Mistakes I Made at Work*《我在工作所犯的錯誤》

Step 1　題目是詢問有些畢業生對於自己初入職場時要求很高,這個出發點是好的,但是它的影響層面是很廣的。首段中先簡短的定義,並表明出進入有名的公司工作並賺取薪資等並沒有任何不對之處。

Step 2　次段拉回主題,提到畢業生對於自己要求過於高,進一步以暢銷書《關鍵性十年》中丹尼爾的例子闡述。丹尼爾將自己跟有經驗且資深的相比,這造成了題目所說的,以及

首段句尾的陳述，對她或畢業生的內心產生了極大的傷害，而摧毀自己本身的信心和內心的不健康，她其實沒有這麼差。

Step 3　接著，進一步論述到想要交出與資深同事同品質的作品是好事，但不要訂下過於高的目標，例如幾天內就要達到。

Step 4　末段提到了，有些公司都有蜜月期，另外進一步地以《我在工作所犯的錯誤》中露絲的觀點做結尾，你不用對自己要求太高。最後提及自己對這整件事情的立場，結束這題的作文。

經由先前的演練後，現在請看整篇範文並聆聽音檔

To be successful is just a part of our human nature. Most university graduates are making lots of preparation during four years of their undergraduate study in the hope of getting in the prestigious company and earning a significantly high salary. There is nothing wrong with the pursuit, but some are making it to be quite damaging to their health and career.

成功僅是我們人性的一部份。大多數的大學畢業生在四年的大學學習期間就做了許多的準備，希望有朝一日能夠進入享譽盛名的公司工作，而且賺取高額的薪資。追求這樣的目標並沒有錯，但是有些卻使得他們本身的健康和職涯遭受相當大的損害。

University graduates are just doing their first job and somehow, they are so hard on themselves. The incentive is always good because they want to do things that can wow the client or their employer, but they are just the beginner. They are just starting to learn things. In *The Defining Decade*, the case of Danielle illustrates this phenomenon, and actually it is worse. "In fact, most of the people she compared herself to were older than she was or had been working longer than she had." This has aroused the issue of being too hard on yourself. It can harm one's health for quite a bit. The heroine Danielle even compares herself to experienced colleagues. It is good that you want to look up to experienced co-workers who do the job well, but at the same time you need to adjust yourself that they have had a few years of experience in doing those tasks. You can gradually deliver the quality of the work very much the same as theirs, but you do not have to set a too high standard that you want to do that in just a few days. Being overly ambitious can ruin your ability to do the work. In some instances, newly recruits quit the job because they think they are lagging behind their co-workers.

大學畢業生才剛開始做他們第一份工作，而不知怎麼的，他們對自己要求很嚴苛。有這樣的動機總是好的，因為他們想要做那些能夠驚艷客戶或他們雇主的事情，但是他們還僅是初學者。他們才剛開始學習事物。在《關鍵性十年》，丹尼爾的例子闡明了這樣的現象，而實際上更糟。「事實上，大多數她與之相比較的人，都比她更年長或是在這個行業工作遠比她長久」。這引起了對自己本身太嚴苛的議題。此舉對於一個人的健康有相當程度的傷害。女主角丹尼爾甚至將她自己與具經驗的同事比較。你想要向有經驗且把份內工作都做好的同事看齊是件好事，但與此同時，你需要調適自我，因為他們在做那些任務時已經有了幾年的工作經驗了。你能夠逐漸交出像那些同事同樣品質的作品，但是你不需要設定太過高的標準，像是你要在幾天內就追趕上他們。過於具有野心可能也會影響你做那份工作的能力。而有些例子，新聘人員辭掉工作因為他們認為自己遠落後於他們的同事。

To be honest, no one expects you to do things right in the first time. Even some companies have a honeymoon of 3 months for you to adjust. In *Mistakes I Made at Work*, Ruth Reichl shares her wisdom that "don't expect too much of yourself when you are young." Sometimes certain kinds of tasks do require years of experience and it is for elder experienced employees who have worked in the industry for more than 10 years. Of course, you do not have to compare yourselves to them, undermine your confidence or minimize your role in the team. Under most circumstances, you just have to do your part right. To sum up, from the above mentioned descriptions, I do think young university graduates should not be too hard on themselves.

說實話，沒有人期待你在第一次就把事情做好，甚至有些公司有三個月的蜜月期讓你去調適。在《我在工作所犯的錯誤》，露絲・雷琪分享了她的智慧「當你還年輕時，別對自己期待太高」。有時候特定的任務確實需要幾年的經驗，而年長有經驗的員工已經在該領域做了超過十年了。當然，你沒有必要去跟他們比較，貶低自己的信心或減損你在團隊中的角色。在大多數的情況下，你只要把你的部分做好即可。總之，從上述提及的敘述，我認為年輕的畢業生不應該對他們自己太過嚴苛。

Part 1
雅思寫作 Task1：精選高分字彙

Part 2
雅思寫作 Task1：圖表題小作文

Part 3
雅思寫作 Task2：大作文

UNIT 10

「拖延」到底是好事還是壞事呢？「拖延」對於人生有可能是有正面意義的嗎？

📖 Writing Task 2 ▶ *MP3 033*

TOPIC

Most people have a negative feeling when it comes to the term procrastination. In the workplace, procrastination makes things delayed and harms the operation of the company. In life, procrastination makes our life miserable and messy because things do not go according to the plan. But do you think procrastination can be a good thing? Use specific examples and explain.

Write at least 250 words

整合能力強化 ❶ 實際演練

請搭配左頁的題目和並構思和完成大作文的演練。

_____

_____

_____

_____

_____

_____

_____

_____

_____

_____

_____

_____

_____

_____

_____

_____

_____

Part 1
雅思寫作 Task1：精選高分字彙

Part 2
雅思寫作 Task1：圖表題小作文

Part 3
雅思寫作 **Task2**：大作文

在掌握文法句型後，學習者大多能拿到 7 分以上的寫作成績，英語句型多樣性是獲取高分的關鍵，現在請演練接下來的單句中譯英練習。請務必演練後再觀看答案，也可以搭配範文音檔強化對各句型的記憶。

❶ 拖延對於大多數的公司來說是很大的阻礙，因為有些任務是有緊湊的截止日期的。

_____

_____

【參考答案】

Procrastination is a great hindrance for most companies since some tasks have a tight deadline.

❷ 效率，另一方面，是大多數高階主管所偏好的，因為他們總想要事情能夠提前完成，這樣一來他們就會某種程度上感到如釋重負。

_____

_____

【參考答案】

Efficiency, on the other hand, is what most executives favor since they all want things to finish earlier so that they will feel relieved somehow.

❸ 當然，沒有人想要拖延因為這樣會表示著有特定的事情尚未完成，有個重擔壓在你身上。

【參考答案】

Of course, no one wants to procrastinate because there is going to be a burden weighing on you that certain things have not done it yet.

❹ 這就是為什麼在公司裡，我們總是想要事情在遠比所訂的期限內快完成，這樣我們就不用有那麼多的焦慮感。

【參考答案】

That is why in the company, we all want things done far ahead of the schedule so that we do not have so much anxiety.

❺ 在《我在工作中所犯的錯誤》，露絲・歐潔琪分享了她的智慧，「拖延將阻礙你充分享受你自己的生活，取而代之的是，該學習如何欣賞自己本身的過錯」。

【參考答案】

In *Mistakes I Made at Work*, Ruth Ozeki shares her wisdom that "Procrastination will prevent you from fully living your life;

instead learn to appreciate your mistakes."

❻ 拖延影響不僅是工作上的事情還包含我們自己的生活。每件小事情，範圍從清理廚房到剪完頭髮。

_____

_____

【參考答案】
Procrastination influences not just things at work but our own life. Every little thing ranging from getting the kitchen cleaned to getting the haircut done.

❼ 儘管所有關於拖延的負面評論，拖延並不總是件壞事情。在《創新》，「拖延對於原創性可能是有益處的」。

_____

_____

【參考答案】
Despite all the negative comments about procrastination, procrastination is not always a bad thing. In *Originals*, "procrastination might be conducive to originality."

❽ 當事情必須要在那麼趕的情況下完成，你不能預期事情能做得多好，而且在製作過程中，一定會有幾個錯誤產生。

_____

_____

【參考答案】

When things have to get done in such a rush, you cannot expect it to be too great, and during the process, there are bound to be several errors made.

❾ 儘管那些錯誤不會被非專業人士所察覺，製作者可能會有個感覺，就是它本可以是件完美的作品。

_____

_____

【參考答案】

Although those mistakes are not going to be detected by non-experts, producers might have the feeling that it could have been an impeccable work.

❿ 稍後的後悔並無助於整件事情，因為結果已經在那了。

_____

_____

【參考答案】

Regretting later won't help the whole thing because the outcome is there.

TOPIC

Most people have a negative feeling when it comes to the term procrastination. In the workplace, procrastination makes things delayed and harms the operation of the company. In life, procrastination makes our life miserable and messy because things do not go according to the plan. But do you think procrastination can be a good thing? Use specific examples and explain.

搭配的暢銷書

- *Mistakes I Made at Work*《我在工作中所犯的錯誤》
- *Originals*《創新》

Step 1 題目詢問了延遲被視為是負面的，因為其造成了進度拖延且影響效率，而值得令人深思的是，延遲對於一件事情的完成等是否能是正面且有助益的呢？首句先定義了關於延遲，次句用了 on the other hand 表現出反差，並講述延遲是與 efficiency 相對之概念。首段結尾以暢銷書《我在工作中所犯的錯誤》中露絲提出的看法，此看法仍是負面的。

Step 2　次段提到影響延遲是有很多因素的，也提到會影響到生活層面的事物。接著提到**拖延並不總是件壞事情**。在《創新》，「拖延對於原創性可能是有益處的」。**將論點拉到其實拖延對於創新是有益處的。**

Step 3　下一個段落提到，在趕進度的情況下，是容易出錯的，並緊接表明出「儘管那些錯誤不會被非專業人士所察覺…」，其實間接表明出這其實是能夠避免的。

Step 4　末段仍提到暢銷書《創新》，提到拖延對於創意是件好事。好的作品是需要時間來完成的，最後巧妙的以「我不認為我必須要把事情看得太嚴肅。每件事總有好的和不好的一面，而拖延碰巧是其中一個。」這個結尾是很棒的，**因為太多事物，都被歸列成非黑即白，但其實並不總是如此，事物通常具有一體兩面**，所以很多時候看事情太絕對，其實不是好事。

經由先前的演練後，現在請看整篇範文並聆聽音檔

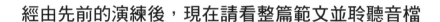

Procrastination is a great hindrance for most companies since some tasks have a tight deadline. Efficiency, on the other hand, is what most executives favor since they all want things to finish earlier so that they will feel relieved somehow. Of course, no one wants to procrastinate because there is going to be a burden weighing on you that certain things have not done it yet. That is why in the company, we all want things done far ahead of the schedule so that we do not have so much anxiety. In *Mistakes I Made at Work*, Ruth Ozeki shares her wisdom that "Procrastination will prevent you from fully living your life; instead learn to appreciate your mistakes."

拖延對於大多數的公司來說是很大的阻礙，因為有些任務是有緊湊的截止日期的。效率，另一方面，是大多數高階主管所偏好的，因為他們總想要事情能夠提前完成，這樣一來他們就會某種程度上感到如釋重負。當然，沒有人想要拖延，因為這樣會表示著有特定的事情尚未完成，有個重擔壓在你身上。這就是為什麼在公司裡，我們總是想要事情在遠比所訂的期限內快完成，這樣我們就不用有那麼多的焦慮感。在《我在工作中所犯的錯誤》，露絲・歐潔琪分享了她的智慧，「拖延將阻礙你充分享受你自己的生活，取而代之的是，該學習如何欣賞自己本身的過錯」。

There are lots of reasons that affect why people procrastinate. Procrastination influences not just things at work but our own life. Every little thing ranging from getting the kitchen cleaned to getting the haircut done. Despite all the negative comments about procrastination, procrastination is not always a bad thing. In *Originals*, "procrastination might be conducive to originality."

有很多因素影響人們為何拖延。拖延影響不僅是工作上的事情還包含我們自己的生活。每件小事情，範圍從清理廚房到剪完頭髮。儘管所有關於拖延的負面評論，拖延並不總是件壞事情。在《創新》，「拖延對於原創性可能是有益處的」。

When things have to get done in such a rush, you cannot expect it to be too great, and during the process, there are bound to be several errors made. Although those mistakes are not going to be detected by non-experts, producers might have the feeling that it could have been an impeccable work. Regretting later won't help the whole thing because the outcome is there.

當事情必須要在那麼趕的情況下完成，你不能預期事情能做得多好，而且在製作過程中，一定會有幾個錯誤產生。儘管那些錯誤不會被非專業人士所察覺，製作者可能會有個感覺，就是它本可以是件完美的作品。稍後的後悔並無助於整件事情，因為結果已經在那了。

In *Originals*, it even states the fact that "procrastination may be the enemy of productivity, but it can be a resource of creativity." Creativity will even make the product more appealing to consumers, especially art works. The author mentions the Mona Lisa as an example to show that Leonardo procrastinated for this incredible thing to be produced. Creative works do take time to be produced. This has provided a great insight for most of us that procrastination can actually be a good thing. Having the time to reflect on things or letting the brain shut down for a significant portion of time can make the result more valuable and rewarding. To sum up, from the above-mentioned descriptions, I do not think we have to view things as being too rigid. Everything has its good side and bad side, and procrastination happens to be one.

在《創新》，它甚至述說了「拖延可能是生產力的敵人，但卻是創意的來源」。創意甚至能夠讓產品在消費者眼中更具有吸引力，尤其是藝術品。作者提到蒙娜麗莎為例，去展示出李奧納多因為拖延才產出了這麼驚人的作品。具創意的作品確實是需要時間來製作的。這已經提供了很偉大的洞察給我們大多數的人，拖延確實是件好事。有時間去反思事情或讓大腦能夠關閉一大段時間，讓結果更具有價值且更值得。總之，從上述提到的描述，我不認為我必須要把事情看得太嚴肅。每件事總有好的和不好的一面，而拖延碰巧是其中一個。

個人特質影響一個人是否能獲取
成功，而就「聰明」跟「大膽」
而言，哪個特質更重要呢？

Writing Task 2 ▶ *MP3 035*

TOPIC

Traits can shape a person. Traits are important because they can determine whether a person can succeed or not, and whether there are so many characteristics, such as honesty, wisdom, cleverness, and boldness. If we narrow down the traits to two, boldness and smartness, do you think which one is more important than the other? Use specific examples and explain.

Write at least 250 words

整合能力強化 ❶ 實際演練

請搭配左頁的題目和並構思和完成大作文的演練。

_____

_____

_____

_____

_____

_____

_____

_____

_____

_____

_____

_____

_____

_____

_____

_____

_____

_____

整合能力強化 ❷ 單句中譯英演練

在掌握文法句型後，學習者大多能拿到 7 分以上的寫作成績，英語句型多樣性是獲取高分的關鍵，現在請演練接下來的單句中譯英練習。請務必演練後再觀看答案，也可以搭配範文音檔強化對各句型的記憶。

❶ 「通常在真實世界裡，不是聰明的人獲得成功，反而是具膽識者。」這句源於《窮爸爸富爸爸》的話，似乎完全回應了關於哪個特質更為重要的這個問題。

_____

_____

【參考答案】

"Often in the real world, it's not the smart who get ahead, but the bold." This line from *Rich Dad Poor Dad* pretty much answers the question about which characteristic is more important.

❷ 在處理特定的任務時，聰明可能給人們確切的優勢進而佔上風，但是那些事情是很瑣碎的。

_____

_____

【參考答案】

Smartness might give people a certain edge to prevail in certain tasks, but those things are trivial.

❸ 在最後，終究歸咎於你是否足夠勇敢，進而採取特定的對策。即
使你不具備某種程度的聰明，而實情是你願意跨越過舒適圈，並
執行它。

_____

_____

【參考答案】

In the end, it all comes down to whether you are gallant enough to
make a certain move. Even if you do not possess a certain level of
smartness, the thing is you are willing to go beyond the comfort
zone and do it.

❹ 聰明的人可能對於整件事情過度思考了，而聰明但不具備膽識的
人仍停留在原地，甚至連一寸都聞風不動，而具膽識的人冒險進
入了一個嶄新的領域，並且讓這些產生了很大程度的不同。

_____

_____

【參考答案】

Smart people might overthink about the whole thing, and smart
people without the courage to do things are still in the same spot,
not moving for even an inch, whereas bold people venture into a
new territory and that makes a huge difference.

❺ 在《但願當我 20 歲時就知道的事》，它談到了「這個世界區分
成，在等待別人的許可去做他們想要從事的事情，以及自己給予
自己許可去做事情的人」。

Part 1
雅思寫作 Task1：精選高分字彙

Part 2
雅思寫作 Task1：圖表題小作文

Part 3
雅思寫作 Task2：大作文

223

_____

_____

【參考答案】

In *What I Wish I Knew When I was 20*, it talks about "The world is divided into people who wait for others to give them permission to do the things they want to do and people who grant themselves permission."

❻ 千真萬確的是大多數的人不敢邁出大膽之舉,而且他們正等待別人給予許可權,像是書中所描述的情況一樣。

_____

_____

【參考答案】

It is true that most people do not dare to make the bold move and they are waiting for the permission like what the book describes.

❼ 當人們質疑你如何能夠創立一間公司,因為你僅是個員工,聰明的人有點退縮了,並且仍舊待在原來的公司當個員工。

_____

_____

【參考答案】

When people are doubting how can you start a company because you are just an employee, smart people shrink for a bit and remain as the employee of the company.

❽ 他們沒有採取任何行動，而反觀具膽識的人卻不在乎其他人怎麼
想的。這並不是說他們變得不理性了。

　　　　　　　　　　　　　　　　　　　　　　　　　　　　　　

　　　　　　　　　　　　　　　　　　　　　　　　　　　　　　

【參考答案】

They do not make the move, while bold people do not care what
others think about. It is not that they are being irrational.

❾ 他們已經對於整件事情做出了評估，這樣一來他們就能夠採取行
動了。即使他們還僅是員工，他們的膽識給予他們足夠的勇氣去
做這件事情。

　　　　　　　　　　　　　　　　　　　　　　　　　　　　　　

　　　　　　　　　　　　　　　　　　　　　　　　　　　　　　

【參考答案】

They have evaluated the whole thing so that they make such a
move. Even though they are just an employee, their boldness
gives them enough courage to do it.

❿ 我已經在這間公司五年了，而且我對於所有這些程序和許多重要
的戰略性商業決策都很熟悉了。

　　　　　　　　　　　　　　　　　　　　　　　　　　　　　　

　　　　　　　　　　　　　　　　　　　　　　　　　　　　　　

【參考答案】

I have been in this company for 5 years and I have already
familiar with all the procedures and many important strategic
business decisions.

225

TOPIC

Traits can shape a person. Traits are important because they can determine whether a person can succeed or not, and whether there are so many characteristics, such as honesty, wisdom, cleverness, and boldness. If we narrow down the traits to two, boldness and smartness, do you think which one is more important than the other? Use specific examples and explain.

搭配的暢銷書

- *Rich Dad Poor Dad*《窮爸爸富爸爸》
- *What I Wish I Knew When I was 20*《但願當我 20 歲時就知道的事》

Step 1　這是關於個人特質的題目，其實是蠻靈活的考題，在口說或寫作中，有時候會出現，可以認真思考下哪些特質對自己而言是最重要的。但題目有限定在兩個特質的討論，所以要針對這兩個特質，選出一個適合的，範文中選了 boldness，如果你選擇 smartness 就可以想下相關搭配的點是什麼。首段很清楚的使用了暢銷書《窮爸爸富爸爸》破題。

Step 2　　次段則討論兩種特點的優缺點，進一步推論出，如果沒有
足夠勇氣邁開那步，就算再聰明也無法達到該目標。

Step 3　　下個段落提到了另一本暢銷書《但願當我 20 歲時就知道的
事》，而確實是如此，有太多的人需要有周遭的人認同並
給予允許才敢做某些事情，**但其他具有膽識者早就去執行
了，這就是兩者間的差異**。然後進一步說明了在公司裡兩
種類型的人在累積的資歷後，具膽識者可能已經創立了一
間公司了，對比差異處。

Step 4　　末段總結出具膽識者更容易獲取成功，而接續以暢銷書
《窮爸爸富爸爸》結尾。

Part 1
雅思寫作 Task1：精選高分字彙

Part 2
雅思寫作 Task1：圖表題小作文

Part 3
雅思寫作 Task2：大作文

經由先前的演練後，現在請看整篇範文並聆聽音檔

"Often in the real world, it's not the smart who get ahead, but the bold." This line from *Rich Dad Poor Dad* pretty much answers the question about which characteristic is more important. Boldness outshines smartness, but why?

「通常在真實世界裡，不是聰明的人獲得成功，反而是具膽識者。」這句源於《窮爸爸富爸爸》的話，似乎完全回應了關於哪個特質更為重要的這個問題。膽識使聰明相形見拙，但是這又是為什麼呢？

Smartness might give people a certain edge to prevail in certain tasks, but those things are trivial. In the end, it all comes down to whether you are gallant enough to make a certain move. Even if you do not possess a certain level of smartness, the thing is you are willing to go beyond the comfort zone and do it. Smart people might overthink about the whole thing, and smart people without the courage to do things are still in the same spot, not moving for even an inch, whereas bold people venture into a new territory and that makes a huge difference.

在處理特定的任務時，聰明可能給人們確切的優勢進而佔上風，但是那些事情是很瑣碎的。在最後，終究歸咎於你是否足夠勇敢，進而採取特定的對策。即使你不具備某種程度的聰明，而實情是你願意跨越過舒適圈，並執行它。聰明的人可能對於整件事情過度思考了，而聰明但不具備膽識的人仍停留在原地，甚至連一寸都聞風不動，而具膽識的人冒險進入了一個嶄新的領域，並且讓這些產生了很大程度的不同。

In *What I Wish I Knew When I was 20*, it talks about "The world is divided into people who wait for others to give them permission to do the things they want to do and people who grant themselves permission." It is true that most people do not dare to make the bold move and they are waiting for the permission like what the book describes. Bold people, on the other hand, do not wait for the permission of others. They do not need any permission. When people are doubting how can you start a company because you are just an employee, smart people shrink for a bit and remain as the employee of the company. They do not make the move, while bold people do not care what others think about. It is not that they are being irrational. They have evaluated the whole thing so that they make such a move. Even though they are just an employee, their boldness gives them enough courage to do it. When faced with all the doubts, they are like why not, I have been in this company for 5 years and I have already familiar with all the procedures and many important strategic business decisions.

在《但願當我 20 歲時就知道的事》，它談到了「這個世界區分成，在等待別人的許可去做他們想要從事的事情，以及自己給予自己許可去做事情的人」。千真萬確的是，大多數的人不敢邁出大膽之舉，而且他們正等待別人給予許可權，像是書中所描述的情況一樣。大膽之人，另一方面，不等待其他人給予許可。他們不需要任何許可。當人們質疑你如何能夠創立一間公司，因為你僅是個員工，聰明的人有點退縮了，並且仍舊待在原來的公司當個員工。他們沒有採取任何行動，而反觀具膽識的人卻不在乎其他人怎麼想的。這並不是說他們變得不理性了。他們已經對於整件事情做出了評估，這樣一來他們就能夠採取行動了。即使他們還僅是員工，他們的膽識給予他們足夠的勇氣去做這件事情。當面臨所有質疑時，他們的反應是為什麼不呢，我已經在這間公司五年了，而且我對於所有這些程序和許多重要的戰略性商業決策都很熟悉了。

There is no reason to stop just because someone has doubts. They are more likely to be successful in the long term, whereas smart people use their smartness in the same company earning the meager salary. Bold people, on the contrary, might start a company and be someone else's boss and earn lots of money. Of course, it comes with the risk. But just like what's in the *Rich Dad Poor Dad*, "Winners are not afraid of losing. But losers are." To sum up, from the above mentioned statements, I do think boldness outshines smartness.

沒有理由停下，難道僅因為一些人對這些事情有些質疑嗎？長遠來看，他們更可能成功，而聰明的人運用了他們聰明在同間公司賺取微薄的薪水。反觀，大膽的人可能開創了一間公司，而成了有些人的老闆了，並賺取許多錢。當然，伴隨而之的是風險。但是這就像是《窮爸爸富爸爸》，「贏家不害怕輸，但是魯蛇卻害怕輸」。總之，從上述的陳述，我認為大膽遠勝過聰明。

UNIT 12

你是否贊成去澳洲打工呢？對於赴澳打工你有什麼具體的建議嗎？

📖 **Writing Task 2** ▶ *MP3 037*

TOPIC

Nowadays, people have multiple options when they are out of the college. They do not necessarily have to work first. Some have chosen a more different approach by having a working holiday in Australia. Are you in favor of the idea, and what suggestions can you give to people who want to go there? Use specific examples and explain.

Write at least 250 words

整合能力強化 ❶ 實際演練

請搭配左頁的題目和並構思和完成大作文的演練。

_____

_____

_____

_____

_____

_____

_____

_____

_____

_____

_____

_____

_____

_____

_____

_____

Part 1
雅思寫作 Task1：精選高分字彙

Part 2
雅思寫作 Task1：圖表題小作文

Part 3
雅思寫作 Task2：大作文

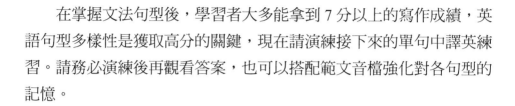

整合能力強化 ❷ 單句中譯英演練

在掌握文法句型後，學習者大多能拿到 7 分以上的寫作成績，英語句型多樣性是獲取高分的關鍵，現在請演練接下來的單句中譯英練習。請務必演練後再觀看答案，也可以搭配範文音檔強化對各句型的記憶。

❶ 許多因素激起那些畢業生前往澳洲尋找他們內心自我。生命必須要有意義和目的，如果那給予他們意義和多采多姿的回憶，我全然同意到澳洲打工渡假的想法。

_____

_____

【參考答案】

Life has to have meanings and purposes, if that gives them meanings and wonderful memories, I totally agree the idea of doing a working holiday in Australia.

❷ 然而，我認為大多數的 20 幾歲的人需要了解到的事實是，這對他們任何一個人來說都是非常重要的決定。

_____

_____

【參考答案】

However, I do think most twentysomethings need to understand the fact that it is a very important decision for any one of them.

❸ 20 幾歲的光陰是形塑對於他們來說更長遠的未來，這遠超乎他們的想像。這並非關於父母的同意，而是關於替他們自己做決定。

_____

_____

【參考答案】

Twentysomething years are what shape their future far ahead and more than they can imagine. It is not about parents' approval but about making the decision for themselves.

❹ 當他們從澳洲回來時，他們真的需要知道他們必須要從頭開始。

_____

_____

【參考答案】

When they come back from Australia, they really need to know that they have to start from scratch.

❺ 對許多雇主來說，他們像是一張白紙沒有任何工作經驗，而當然，那些工作，包含切和解剖牛或是採集草莓，儘管令人感到有趣和好玩，對那些雇主來說不具有任何意義。

_____

_____

【參考答案】

To many employers, they are like a white paper without any work experience, and of course, those works, including slicing and dissecting bulls or gathering strawberries, although they are intriguing and fun, mean nothing to those employers.

❻ 你必須不只要從頭開始,更要有種心理準備,就是你的起薪不會太高。此外,你未赴澳洲的同學,已經累積了幾年的工作經驗了。

_____

_____

【參考答案】

You have to not just start from the scratch but totally have in mind that your first salary won't be that high. Furthermore, your classmates who have not gone to Australia, have already accumulated several years of work experiences.

❼ 這並不是在做比較,但是事實是他們之中的有些人可能已經做到管理職或有更高的薪資了。

_____

_____

【參考答案】

It is not about making comparison, but the truth is some of them might be in the managerial positions or have higher salaries.

❽ 可能會有點遲才意識到那些事情。有時候那些東西對於有些人來說是很傷的。

_____

_____

【參考答案】

It might be a little late to realize the fact about those things. Sometimes those things do hurt a little bit for some people.

❾ 有些人可能實際上到了那裡，並累積了許多金錢，甚至是一百萬元，但是對於金錢你必須要很小心翼翼。

_____

_____

【參考答案】

Some might actually go there and accumulate a lot money, even a million dollars, but you have to be really careful about the money.

❿ 既然錢很難賺，將錢花費在娛樂用途，例如幾次的國際旅行，可能會是個浪費。你將失去你的優勢，因為那些存款能讓你遠遠領有些 20 幾歲的人。

_____

_____

【參考答案】

Since money is hard-earned, utilizing the money for recreational usage, such as taking several international trips might be a waste. You have given your advantage away because with those savings you are far ahead of some twentysomethings.

TOPIC

Nowadays, people have multiple options when they are out of the college. They do not necessarily have to work first. Some have chosen a more different approach by having a working holiday in Australia. Are you in favor of the idea, and what suggestions can you give to people who want to go there? Use specific examples and explain.

Step 1　首段先定義，並且講述大家會想要前往澳洲打工度假的原因。然後表明立場，代表自己是贊同的。然後因為題目有問「提供的建議」，所以可以邊想下兩到三個論點在後面段落中進行鋪陳。範文中提到的是對於返國後找工作和金錢的使用。

Step 2　次段表達出，這對選擇前往澳洲打工度假者是很重大的決定，進一步提到 20 **幾歲的光陰是形塑對於他們來說更長遠的未來，這遠超乎他們的想像。這並非關於父母的同意。**再來，說明站在老闆的角度，對於澳洲打工的工作的看法如何，提到一張白紙和回國後仍要從零開始。另一方面，要面臨起薪仍不高，還有同儕都已位居要職或有較高薪資，是有可能會造成心理不平衡。

Step 3　下一段講到，關於金錢，其實辛苦存下的錢，若揮霍掉其實意義不大，應該要將錢用於其他用途等，那段用體力和青春換取的金錢，要花在更有價值的事情上。（雖然每個人對於錢的使用有不同的看法，但也有許多人揮霍掉後，在中年後感到後悔。）

Step 4　然後總結出，如果對於工作有好的認識以及將錢用於更有價值的事情上，這趟旅程其實更豐富，除了回憶等，還包含了實質的進帳。

經由先前的演練後，現在請看整篇範文並聆聽音檔

Doing a working holiday in Australia is many university graduates' dream whether it is because of the low salary given by multiple companies or whether it is because of the scenery and exotic and dreamy lifestyle. Multiple factors fuel those graduates to Australia in search of their inner self. Life has to have meanings and purposes, if that gives them meanings and wonderful memories, I totally agree the idea of doing a working holiday in Australia.

赴澳洲打工渡假是許多大學畢業生的夢想，不論原因是因為眾多公司都給予低薪或是因為風景和異國風情且夢幻的生活型態。許多因素激起那些畢業生前往澳洲尋找他們內心自我。生命必須要有意義和目的，如果那給予他們意義和多采多姿的回憶，我全然同意到澳洲打工渡假的想法。

However, I do think most twentysomethings need to understand the fact that it is a very important decision for any one of them. Twentysomething years are what shape their future far ahead and more than they can imagine. It is not about parents' approval but about making the decision for themselves. When they come back from Australia, they really need to know that they have to start from scratch. To many employers, they are like a white paper without any work experience, and of course, those works, including slicing and dissecting bulls or gathering strawberries, although they are intriguing and fun, mean nothing to those employers. You have to not just start from the scratch but totally have in mind that your first salary won't be that high. Furthermore, your classmates who have not gone to Australia, have already accumulated several years of work experiences. It is not about making comparison, but the truth is some of them might be in the managerial positions or have higher salaries. It might be a little late to realize the fact about those things. Sometimes those things do hurt a little bit for some people.

然而，我認為大多數的 20 幾歲的人需要了解到的事實是，這對他們任何一個人來說都是非常重要的決定。20 幾歲的光陰是形塑對於他們來說更長遠的未來，這遠超乎他們的想像。這並非關於父母的同意，而是關於替他們自己做決定。當他們從澳洲回來時，他們真的需要知道他們必須要從頭開始。對許多雇主來說，他們像是一張白紙沒有任何工作經驗，而當然，那些工作，包含切和解剖牛或是採集草莓，儘管令人感到有趣和好玩，對那些雇主來說不具有任何意義。你必須不只要從頭開始，更要有種心理準備，就是你的起薪不會太高。此外，你未赴澳洲的同學，已經累積了幾年的工作經驗了。這並不是在做比較，但是事實是他們之中的有些人可能已經做到管理職或有更高的薪資了。可能會有點遲才意識到那些事情。有時候那些東西對於有些人來說是很傷的。

Another thing related to the working holiday in Australia is money. Some might actually go there and accumulate a lot money, even a million dollars, but you have to be really careful about the money. Since money is hard-earned, utilizing the money for recreational usage, such as taking several international trips might be a waste. You have given your advantage away because with those savings you are far ahead of some twentysomethings. You should save it or for the financial plan so that hard-earned money in Australia can be better utilized.

另一件關於澳洲打工的事情是金錢。有些人可能實際上到了那裡，並累積了許多金錢，甚至是一百萬元，但是對於金錢，你必須要很小心翼翼。既然錢很難賺，將錢花費在娛樂用途，例如幾次的國際旅行，可能會是個浪費。你將失去你的優勢，因為那些存款能讓你遠遠領先有些 20 幾歲的人。你應該要存下來或將其用於財務規劃用途，這樣一來在澳洲難賺的錢能有更好的利用。

To sum up, if people doing the working holiday in Australia can have an understanding about work and really manage their hard-earned money, I think going to this trip will not just give them some wonderful memories, but also the edge for their life ahead.

總之，如果人們要到澳洲打工渡假，要有對於工作上的了解，且真正管理好他們辛苦賺取的金錢，我認為這趟旅程不僅會給予他們有些多采多姿的回憶，也會讓他們未來的生活更有優勢。

「成長型思維模式」和「固定型思維模式」對人們的學習和獲取成功影響甚鉅，請以具體實例解釋兩者間的差異。

Writing Task 2 ▶ *MP3 039*

TOPIC

Our thinking matters to us, and it can make or break us. Some are thinking in a narrower way, and they are having a fastened way of thinking, the so-called the fixed mindset. Others have a more flexible thinking approach. They think failures are part of the process and they actually help us to succeed in life. They belong to the growth mindset. Do you think people should all learn both ideas so they can have a more fulfilling life? use specific examples and explain.

Write at least 250 words

整合能力強化 ❶ 實際演練

請搭配左頁的題目和並構思和完成大作文的演練。

在掌握文法句型後，學習者大多能拿到 7 分以上的寫作成績，英語句型多樣性是獲取高分的關鍵，現在請演練接下來的單句中譯英練習。請務必演練後再觀看答案，也可以搭配範文音檔強化對各句型的記憶。

❶ 當賈斯汀，《醜女貝蒂》裡的其中一位角色，拿到入學通知的拒絕信時，他告訴他的家人，他不想要等明年，以及他想要今年就要進他理想的學校就讀。

_____

_____

【參考答案】

When Justin, one of the characters in *Ugly Betty*, gets the rejection letter, he tells his family that he doesn't want next year, and he wants to go to his desired school this year.

❷ 他母親當時的男朋友，一位議員回應了他這個舉動，簡單且值得讚許。

_____

_____

【參考答案】

How his mother's boyfriend, a senator, responds to his reaction, is simple but commendable.

❸ 他說這是需要時間的，而這也是為什麼要花費他數年，他才獲取現在的職位。

_____

_____

【參考答案】

He says it takes time, and this is why it takes him years to get his position now.

❹ 藉由分析他們對於挫折的反應，我們可以很清楚看到賈斯汀是位具有固定型思維模式的人，而議員卻具有成長型思維模式。

_____

_____

【參考答案】

By analyzing how they react to failures, we can clearly see that Justin is someone with a fixed mindset, whereas the senator possesses the growth mindset.

❺ 在《關鍵十年》，它也談論到成長型思維模式的重要性。「對於那些具有成長型思維模式者，失敗可能會讓人感到刺痛，但是他們將其視為是改進和改變的機會」。

_____

_____

【參考答案】

In _The Defining Decade_, it also talks about the importance of the growth mindset. "For those who have a growth mindset, failures may sting but they are also viewed as opportunities for improvement and change."

❽ 在《我在工作中所犯的錯誤》，卡洛斯・德維克提及「當你具有成長型思維模式時，你了解到錯誤和挫折是學習中不可或缺的一部分」。

_____

_____

【參考答案】

In *Mistakes I Made at Work*, Carol S. Dweck mentions "When you have a "growth mindset", you understand that mistakes and setbacks are an inevitable part of learning."

❼ 兩者清楚地顯示出思考模式的重要性，以及這會如何影響到結果。

_____

_____

【參考答案】

Both clearly show the importance of thinking patterns and how it is going to affect the result.

❽ 具有固定型思維模式者，像是賈斯汀這樣的人，似乎無法好好處理挫折，而這或多或少衝擊他們稍後的表現。

_____

_____

【參考答案】

People possessing a fixed mindset, someone like Justin, cannot seem to handle rejections well, and this more or less impacts their later performance.

❾ 因為失敗的經驗，它實際上幫助你修復你內在所欠缺的，而你如何能夠在進行第二次嘗試時，改進事情和做出更好的工作成果。

_____

_____

【參考答案】

Because of the failing experience, it actually helps you to remedy what is clearly lacking inside you, and how you can improve things and do a better job in the second attempt.

❿ 一旦你的思考模式已經從固定型思維模式轉換到成長型思維模式，你將發現，生活簡單多了，而成功總是近在直呎。

_____

_____

【參考答案】

Once your thinking patterns have changed from a fixed mindset to a growth mindset, you will find life is a lot easier and success is always near.

TOPIC

Our thinking matters to us, and it can make or break us. Some are thinking in a narrower way, and they are having a fastened way of thinking, the so-called the fixed mindset. Others have a more flexible thinking approach. They think failures are part of the process and they actually help us to succeed in life. They belong to the growth mindset. Do you think people should all learn both ideas so they can have a more fulfilling life? use specific examples and explain.

搭配的暢銷書

- *The Defining Decade*《關鍵十年》
- *Mistakes I Made at Work*《我在工作中所犯的錯誤》

Step 1　題目是關於兩種思維模式：**成長型思維模式**和**固定型思維模式**，常見的敘述手法較難寫出好的論點。首段以很引人入勝的手法切入，是上乘的佳作。藉由影集中人物帶入主題，而非一堆陳述句和定義，讓讀者能接續閱讀下去，並從影集中兩位人物比較出要介紹的兩的觀點：**賈斯汀 (fixed mindset)** 和**議員 (Growth mindset)**

Step 2　次段以另外兩本暢銷書解釋和定義這兩個思維模式的差異，是很具體的表達，從中可以很明顯的了解到思考模式影響到成果。**成長型思維模式者將其視為是改進和改變的機會，而且了解到錯誤和挫折是學習中不可或缺的一部分，這也是他們更能成功的原因。**

Step 3　下一段，經由上一段的解釋跟進一步的定義後，再回來談論剛剛兩位主角並做出總結，也是藉由比較得出結論，推論出「你就具備了成功的特質，而且你不用因為失敗的嘗試被擊倒。一旦你的思考模式已經從固定型思維模式轉換到成長型思維模式，你將發現，生活簡單多了，而成功總是近在直呎。最後說明我們都該要對這兩個思考模式有認識，這對我們生活中有幫助。

Part 1
雅思寫作 Task1：精選高分字彙

Part 2
雅思寫作 Task1：圖表題小作文

Part 3
雅思寫作 Task2：大作文

經由先前的演練後，現在請看整篇範文並聆聽音檔

When Justin, one of the characters in *Ugly Betty*, gets the rejection letter, he tells his family that he doesn't want next year, and he wants to go to his desired school this year. How his mother's boyfriend, a senator, responds to his reaction, is simple but commendable. He says it takes time, and this is why it takes him years to get his position now. By analyzing how they react to failures, we can clearly see that Justin is someone with a fixed mindset, whereas the senator possesses the growth mindset.

當賈斯汀，《醜女貝蒂》裡的其中一位角色，拿到入學通知的拒絕信時，他告訴他的家人，他不想要等明年，以及他想要今年就要進他理想的學校就讀。他母親當時的男朋友，一位議員回應了他這個舉動，簡單且值得讚許。他說這是需要時間的，而這也是為什麼要花費他數年，他才獲取現在的職位。藉由分析他們對於挫折的反應，我們可以很清楚看到賈斯汀是位具有固定型思維模式的人，而議員卻具有成長型思維模式。

The two following bestsellers also discusses the concept of the growth mindset. In *The Defining Decade*, it also talks about the importance of the growth mindset. "For those who have a growth mindset, failures may sting but they are also viewed as opportunities for improvement and change." In *Mistakes I Made at Work*, Carol S. Dweck mentions "When you have a "growth mindset", you understand that mistakes and setbacks are an inevitable part of learning." Both clearly show the importance of thinking patterns and how it is going to affect the result.

下列兩位暢銷書作者也討論到了成長型思維模式的觀念。在《關鍵十年》，它也談論到成長型思維模式的重要性。「對於那些具有成長型思維模式者，失敗可能會讓人感到刺痛，但是他們將其視為是改進和改變的機會」。在《我在工作中所犯的錯誤》，卡洛斯・德維克提及「當你具有成長型思維模式時，你了解到錯誤和挫折是學習中不可或缺的一部分」。兩者清楚地顯示出思考模式的重要性，以及這會如何影響到結果。

People possessing a fixed mindset, someone like Justin, cannot seem to handle rejections well, and this more or less impacts their later performance. They can view things as this is too hard to accomplish, and the thinking pattern is set. They think they are never going to make it. But to people who have the growth mindset, they see things differently. They see things as something that really takes some time and effort to get there. They are not defeated to a first no, and in fact it is true that most people do not get the desired result in their first attempt. In life, you have to value failures as the nutrition for growth. Because of the failing experience, it actually helps you to remedy what is clearly lacking inside you, and how you can improve things and do a better job in the second attempt. If you view things like this, you have possessed the quality for success, and you won't feel quashed by failed attempts. Once your thinking patterns have changed from a fixed mindset to a growth mindset, you will find life is a lot easier and success is always near. To sum up, from the above mentioned descriptions, I think we should really know the difference between a fixed mindset and a growth mindset so that we can have a more satisfying life.

具有固定型思維模式者，像是賈斯汀這樣的人，似乎無法好好處理挫折，而這或多或少衝擊他們稍後的表現。他們可以將事情看成是過難而無法達成，而這樣的思考模式就定型了。他們認為他們無法達成。但是對於有著思考型思維模式者，他們看事情的角度卻是截然不同。他們把事情看成是一些真的需要時間和努力去達到的。他們不會因為第一次的拒絕而被擊倒，而事實上，這是千真萬確的，大多數的人並沒有在首次嘗試時就達到理想的結果。在生命中，你必須要將失敗當成是成長的養分。因為失敗的經驗，它實際上幫助你修復你內在所欠缺的，而你如何能夠在進行第二次嘗試時，改進事情和做出更好的工作成果。如果你把事情看成是這樣的話，你就具備了成功的特質，而且你不用因為失敗的嘗試被擊倒。一旦你的思考模式已經從固定型思維模式轉換到成長型思維模式，你將發現，生活簡單多了，而成功總是近在直呎。總之，從上述的描述，我認為我們真的應該要知道固定型思維模式和成長型思維模式，這樣一來我們就可以有更滿足的生活。

許多人嚮往能在工作和生活中取得平衡，是否有能取得工作和生活平衡的工作呢？如果有的話又要如何獲取這樣類型的工作呢？你認為思考的方式有影響嗎？請以具體實例解釋。

Writing Task 2 ▶ MP3 041

TOPIC

The idea of work-life balance is great, and lots of us have sought multiple approaches to get that, but to no avail. Do you think there are actually jobs that can meet the work-life balance criteria. If so what are those and how to get the kind of job. Do you think ways of thinking matter? Use specific examples and explain.

Write at least 250 words

許多人嚮往能在工作和生活中取得平衡,是否有能取得工作和生活平衡的工作呢?如果有的話又要如何獲取這樣類型的工作呢?你認為思考的方式有影響嗎?請以具體實例解釋。

🎓 整合能力強化 ❶ 實際演練

請搭配左頁的題目和並構思和完成大作文的演練。

_____

_____

_____

_____

_____

_____

_____

_____

_____

_____

_____

_____

_____

_____

_____

_____

在掌握文法句型後，學習者大多能拿到 7 分以上的寫作成績，英語句型多樣性是獲取高分的關鍵，現在請演練接下來的單句中譯英練習。請務必演練後再觀看答案，也可以搭配範文音檔強化對各句型的記憶。

❶ 在《我工作中所犯的錯誤中》，金・古登提到「工作－生活平衡的想法並不總是有助益」。如果你沉浸在你的工作和養育一個家庭，你可能會感覺到許多好事情 – 但是可能不會包含平衡」。

_____

_____

【參考答案】

In *Mistakes I Made at Work*, Kim Gordon mentions "The idea of "work-life balance" is not necessarily helpful. If you are immersed in your work and raising a family, you might feel a lot of good things – but it may not include balanced."

❷ 這個陳述似乎是告知我們追求工作和生活平衡的工作是不可能的，而這是令人沮喪的。

_____

_____

【參考答案】

The statement seems to inform us that seeking a work-life balance job is so unlikely, and this is so discouraging.

❸ 另一位專家，一位高勝資深經理說道「你越是談論到工作和生活平衡，你越是創造出你想要解決的問題」。

_____

_____

【參考答案】

Another expert, a senior director at Goldman Sachs said "the more you talk about work-life balance, the more you create the problem that you want to solve."

❹ 這進一步地證實了，會有接踵而來的問題，當你看到那樣的工作時。但是工作和生活中平衡的工作是否存在呢？

_____

_____

【參考答案】

This further validates there is going to be an ensuing problem when you see this kind of job. But does the job of work-life balance not exist?

❺ 專家們已經告訴我們的確實是有些根據和洞察性的重點，但是不論專家們告訴我們什麼，工作和生活中取得平衡的工作確實存在著。

_____

_____

【參考答案】

What experts have told us do have some valid and insightful

points, but regardless of what experts tell us, the job of work-life balance does exist.

❻ 這是夢幻工作，而這不是你追求的。這使我們大多數的人感到困惑。但這像是書中所述，「夢幻工作通常是創造出來的，而非找到的」。

_____

_____

【參考答案】

It is the dream job, and it is not something that you seek. This puzzles many of us. But it is like what is described in the book, "dream job is often created than found."

❼ 通常，這不是你在找工作的頁面中會看到的。這可能是個替有些具有不可取代的專業技巧和工作經驗者所打造的，而招募者認為你可以是唯一一個可以做那個工作的人。

_____

_____

【參考答案】

Normally, it is not the job that you see on the job search pages. This could be the job for someone who has irreplaceable technical skills and job experiences, and recruiters deem you can be the one to do the job.

❽ 這份工作是一些具有能力，可能能夠達到公司未來目標者所設計

的。這樣的工作是相當罕見的。

_____

_____

【參考答案】

The job is designed for someone who might have the skill to do things that can meet the future goals of the company. This kind of the job is exceptionally rare.

❾ 有些工作讓你有足夠的彈性，每周的特定幾天你可以經營好你的工作和家庭。

_____

_____

【參考答案】

Some jobs are flexible enough for you to work for certain days a week so that you can manage both your work and your family.

❿ 總之，我認為有著對的思考模式，你可以管理好生活和工作，即使你沒有夢幻工作。

_____

_____

【參考答案】

To sum up, I think with right thinking, you can manage both life and work, even if you do not have the dream job.

整合能力強化 ❸ 段落拓展

TOPIC

The idea of work-life balance is great, and lots of us have sought multiple approaches to get that, but to no avail. Do you think there are actually jobs that can meet the work-life balance criteria. If so what are those and how to get the kind of job. Do you think ways of thinking matter? Use specific examples and explain.

搭配的暢銷書

- *Mistakes I Made at Work* 《我工作中所犯的錯誤中》
- *The Job* 《工作》

Step 1　題目是詢問關於在工作和生活中能取得平衡的工作。這題也不太好答，在缺乏許多實例時，是很難論述跟說服閱讀者。首段先由暢銷書《我工作中所犯的錯誤中》，金提到的看法，並進一步由另一本暢銷書《工作》的觀點，逐步導引出問題，「工作和生活中平衡的工作是否存在呢？」。

Step 2　次段提到在工作和生活中取得平衡的工作確實存在著，並

提及這是夢幻工作，而找到夢幻工作還牽涉到其他條件，主要是表明有這樣的工作存在，但很稀少。

Step 3　下個段落提到，另一類型的工作，能提供求職者彈性工時的工作，這種類型的工作就能平衡工作跟家庭。

Step 4　末段提到思考模式，其實思考影響甚鉅，很神奇的是，當你認為你能做到時，其實你就能做到，但當你覺得你只能擇一時，你人生終究只能擇一，而且你只能遠望別人兩者都擁有。（其實尤其像是在西方社會，有些女生當上高階主管，並同時養育了出色的小孩，同時享有家庭幸福跟職場成功，但也有當上高階主管但卻維持單身者，因為認為自己無法兼顧兩者，其實一開始的思維是否設限就影響蠻大，反而跟其他條件像是學經歷無關了。）

經由先前的演練後，現在請看整篇範文並聆聽音檔

In *Mistakes I Made at Work,* Kim Gordon mentions "The idea of "work-life balance" is not necessarily helpful. If you are immersed in your work and raising a family, you might feel a lot of good things – but it may not include balanced." The statement seems to inform us that seeking a work-life balance job is so unlikely, and this is so discouraging. Another expert, a senior director at Goldman Sachs said "the more you talk about work-life balance, the more you create the problem that you want to solve." This further validates there is going to be an ensuing problem when you see this kind of job. But does the job of work-life balance not exist?

在《我工作中所犯的錯誤中》，金・古登提到「工作－生活平衡的想法並不總是有助益」。如果你沉浸在你的工作和養育一個家庭，你可能會感覺到許多好事情 – 但是可能不會包含平衡」。這個陳述似乎是告知我們追求工作和生活平衡的工作是不可能的，而這是令人沮喪的。另一位專家，一位高勝資深經理說道「你越是談論到工作和生活平衡，你越是創造出你想要解決的問題」。這進一步地證實了，會有接踵而來的問題，當你看到那樣的工作時。但是工作和生活中平衡的工作是否存在呢？

What experts have told us do have some valid and insightful points, but regardless of what experts tell us, the job of work-life balance does exist. It is the dream job, and it is not something that you seek. This puzzles many of us. But it is like what is described in the book, "dream job is often created than found." Normally, it is not the job that you see on the job search pages. This could be the job for someone who has irreplaceable technical skills and job experiences, and recruiters deem you can be the one to do the job. But in the company, they do not have that kind of job title yet. The job is designed for someone who might have the skill to do things that can meet the future goals of the company. This kind of the job is exceptionally rare.

專家們已經告訴我們的確實是有些根據和洞察性的重點，但是不論專家們告訴我們什麼，工作和生活中取得平衡的工作確實

存在著。這是夢幻工作，而這不是你追求的。這使我們大多數
的人感到困惑。但這像是書中所述，「夢幻工作通常是創造出
來的，而非找到的」。通常，這不是你在找工作的頁面中會看
到的。但在公司中尚未有這個頭銜的工作存在。這可能是個替
有些具有不可取代的專業技巧和工作經驗者所打造的，而招募
者認為你是唯一一個可以做那個工作的人。這份工作是一些具
有能力，可能能夠達到公司未來目標者所設計的。這樣的工作
是相當罕見的。

In other occasions, it can be the work-life balance. Jobs
that offer you to have a flexible work mode are the
solution for the problem. Some jobs are flexible enough
for you to work for certain days a week so that you can
manage both your work and your family. Other jobs are
jobs that can be done at home. These jobs are the cure for
someone who has younger kids.

在其他時機，這可以是工作和生活的平衡。工作提供給你彈性
的工作模式是這個問題的解決之道。有些工作讓你有足夠的彈
性，每周的特定幾天你可以經營好你的工作和家庭。其他工作
則是你能夠在家完成的。這些工作都是對於有較年輕的小孩者
的治療之方。

Another thing about the work-life balance is related to thinking patterns. You think you can manage both work and life, then you can do both. If you deem yourself as someone who can manage either work or life, then you can only manage either one. Thinking shapes how one performs. To sum up, I think with right thinking, you can manage both life and work, even if you do not have the dream job. Our will is much powerful than what you think.

另一件關於工作和生活平衡的是關於思考模式。你認為你可能同時經營好工作和生活，那麼你就能做到。如果你認為你自己僅能處理好工作或生活其中之一，那麼你就僅能管理好其中一項。思考形塑一個人如何表現。總之，我認為有著對的思考模式，你可以管理好生活和工作，即使你沒有夢幻工作。我們的意志遠你比想像的要強大的多了。

UNIT 15

年資並非是舊概念，在特定領域耕耘數年就會累積特定的年資，你認為年資重要嗎？年資如何影響一個人在同公司和不同公司呢？年資會影響一個人的職涯嗎？請以具體實例解釋。

Writing Task 2 ▶ *MP3 043*

TOPIC

Seniority is not a novel concept. People working in a specific field for a few years and accumulating work experiences will have the seniority. Do you think seniority matters? How does seniority affect a person in the company they are working for and other companies? Will seniority influence a person's career? Use specific examples and explain.

Write at least 250 words

🎓 整合能力強化 ❶ 實際演練

請搭配左頁的題目和並構思和完成大作文的演練。

_____

_____

_____

_____

_____

_____

_____

_____

_____

_____

_____

_____

_____

_____

_____

　　在掌握文法句型後，學習者大多能拿到 7 分以上的寫作成績，英語句型多樣性是獲取高分的關鍵，現在請演練接下來的單句中譯英練習。請務必演練後再觀看答案，也可以搭配範文音檔強化對各句型的記憶。

❶ 年資像是複利效應一樣，年資的影響可能比你想像中更為深遠，尤其是當你的職涯更有進展時。

_____

_____

【參考答案】

Seniority is like the compound effect, and its influence can be more profound than you think, especially when you career progresses.

❷ 現今，大多數的 20 幾歲的人和 30 幾歲的人並未意識到年資如何影響他們，所以他們做了許多令人感到遺憾的決定。

_____

_____

【參考答案】

Nowadays, most twentysomethings and thirtysomethings are not aware of how seniority will affect them, so they make lots of regrettable decisions.

❸ 回想起來，他們確實沒有時光機能夠修復過去，而過去持續縈繞著他們。

【參考答案】

Looking back, they do not have a time machine to fix the past, and the past keeps haunting them.

❹ 在《窮爸爸富爸爸》，它提到了一個案例，一個人因為不知道年資的重要性而飽受其苦。

【參考答案】

In *Rich Dad Poor Dad*, it mentions a case about the person who suffers from not knowing the importance of seniority.

❺ 「問題是它無法找到對等的工作，認可他從舊公司的年資」。

【參考答案】

"The problem was that he couldn't find an equivalent job that recognized his seniority from the old company."

❻ 這也是個讓我們了解到不是所有公司都以同樣的方式評價年資的

271

案例。工作申請者通常誤解了年資的想法。

_____

_____

It is a case for us to realize that not all companies value the seniority in the same way. Job-applicants often mistake the idea of the seniority.

❼ 他們認為在同間公司的特定領域待了三年就意謂著他們有了三年的工作經驗，但是實際上卻不然。

_____

_____

They think being in the company for three years in a certain area means they are having three years of working experiences, but in fact it is not.

❽ 當他們向頂尖公司申請職位時，對方卻評定你的年資為零。你仍像是個初學者般，就像是大學畢業生剛開始申請第一份工作。

_____

_____

When they apply for a top company, they deem your seniority as zero. You are still starting at the beginning just like college graduates applying for their first jobs.

❾ 頂尖公司會以這樣的方式評估的原因是因為他們是最棒的，而你想要替他們工作，那麼你就必須要遵從他們的評估和規範，進而獲取根據他們所評估的薪資。

_____

_____

【參考答案】

Top companies are evaluating it in this way because they are the great one, and if you want to work for them, then you have to follow their evaluations and norms, and get the salary based on what they estimate.

❿ 也有可能是在你具有三年工作經驗後，你仍需要一個領導者在接下來的六個月帶著你，當他們招募時。

_____

_____

【參考答案】

It is also possible that after your three years of working experiences, you still need a guide for the following six months, when they recruit.

TOPIC

Seniority is not a novel concept. People working in a specific field for a few years and accumulating work experiences will have the seniority. Do you think seniority matters? How does seniority affect a person in the company they are working for and other companies? Will seniority influence a person's career? Use specific examples and explain.

搭配的暢銷書

■ *Rich Dad Poor Dad*《窮爸爸富爸爸》

Step 1　題目是關於年資，當中其實牽涉到許多可以討論到的部分。首段先以「年資像是複利效應一樣」破題，並比喻在 20-30 幾歲的時期，年資確實會影響到一個人後面的發展，是沒有時光機可以重來一次的。

Step 2　次段提到一個《窮爸爸富爸爸》中的案例，離職後因為無法找到能核定對應年資的工作者，而又因為要維持生活基本的開銷，必須要做三份工作。另一方面，進一步闡述誤解年資的概念，許多人誤以為在同間公司工作多久就累積

多少年資，但正確的理解是，在該公司確實如此，但轉換工作到另一間公司時就不是這回事了。其他公司會有其他考量，並舉例出，如果換到頂尖的公司時，還會有核定年資的問題，可能年資會歸零，等同剛畢業求職者，而當中又牽涉到一些因素。

Step 3　最後一段提到也是跟年資有關的事情，是關於解雇老闆，沒有累積一定年資或太常轉換領域，要面臨的就是年資又歸零，等同無法獲得更高的薪資待遇。另一個傷害是，經由那麼多次的轉換仍然不知道自己要什麼，更難獲得面試官的青睞。最後總結出要有正確的態度並要對於年資有所了解。

經由先前的演練後，現在請看整篇範文並聆聽音檔

Seniority is like the compound effect, and its influence can be more profound than you think, especially when you career progresses. Nowadays, most twentysomethings and thirtysomethings are not aware of how seniority will affect them, so they make lots of regrettable decisions. Looking back, they do not have a time machine to fix the past, and the past keeps haunting them.

年資像是複利效應一樣，年資的影響可能比你想像中更為深遠，尤其是當你的職涯更有進展時。現今，大多數的 20 幾歲的人和 30 幾歲的人並未意識到年資如何影響他們，所以他們做了許多令人感到遺憾的決定。回想起來，他們確實沒有時光機能夠修復過去，而過去持續縈繞著他們。

In *Rich Dad Poor Dad*, it mentions a case about the person who suffers from not knowing the importance of seniority. "The problem was that he couldn't find an equivalent job that recognized his seniority from the old company." It is a case for us to realize that not all companies value the seniority in the same way. Job-applicants often mistake the idea of the seniority. They think being in the company for three years in a certain area means they are having three years of working experiences, but in fact it is not. When they apply for a top company, they deem your seniority as zero. You are still starting at the beginning just like college graduates applying for their first jobs. Top companies are evaluating it in this way because they are the great ones, and if you want to work for them, then you have to follow their evaluations and norms, and get the salary based on what they estimate. It is also possible that after your three years of working experiences, you still need a guide for the following six months, when they recruit.

在《窮爸爸富爸爸》，它提到了一個案例，一個人因為不知道年資的重要性而飽受其苦。「問題是他無法找到對等的工作，認可他從舊公司的年資」。這也是個讓我們了解到不是所有公司都以同樣的方式評價年資的案例。工作申請者通常誤解了年資的想法。他們認為在同間公司的特定領域待了三年就意謂著他們有了三年的工作經驗，但是實際上卻不然。當他們向頂尖公司申請職位時，對方卻評定你的年資為零。你仍像是個初學者般，就像是大學畢業生剛開始申請第一份工作。頂尖公司會以這樣的方式評估的原因是因為他們是最棒的，而你想要替他們工作，那麼你就必須要遵從他們的評估和規範，進而獲取根據他們所評估的薪資。也有可能是在你具有三年工作經驗後，你仍需要一個領導者在接下來的六個月帶著你，當他們招募時。

Another thing related to the seniority is a more serious one. Some job-applicants deem this as the fun thing to do. They fire their boss very often, and they work in several different industries, but the thing is they do not have the seniority. When they apply for another job in a new industry, they are still the rookie. Their salaries are still based on the evaluation that has no experience. Without the seniority, it is highly unlikely to get a decent or high salary. It is even less fun when you are after thirty years old. In life, you just cannot afford too many times of starting from the very beginning. This makes some interviewees hard to get a job, since HR personnel might evaluate you in a certain way. Like after five or six attempts from your previous jobs, you still have not figured out what you want to do. Then it is impossible for them to recruit you. To sum up, we all need to have the right mindset when it comes to work, and knowing the concept about seniority is very important.

另一件與年資有關的事情是更嚴重的事。有些工作求職者認為這是有趣的事情。他們很常解僱他們的老闆，而他們在幾個不同的產業工作，但是他們不具有年資。當他們申請到一個新的產業的工作時，他們仍舊是菜鳥。他們的薪資仍是基於不具工作經驗所得來的評估。沒有年資，極不可能獲取相當或高額的薪資。當你 30 歲後這甚至更不好玩了。在生活中，你沒辦法經得起許多次歸零的從頭開始。這也使得許多面試者們更難獲取一份工作了，既然人事專員可能以特定的方式去評估你。像是你之前工作都經過五到六次的嘗試，你仍然不瞭解你自己想要做什麼。那麼他們更不可能去錄用你。總之，我們都需要有對的態度，當提及工作時，而知道一些關於年資的概念是非常重要的。

許多畢業生大學畢業後都有學貸，有些甚至需要在高中兼職打工。你認為學生該享受當下還是儘管家庭財務狀況許可，仍要打工呢？這對他們的未來有什麼影響呢？請以具體實例解釋。

Writing Task 2 ▶ MP3 045

TOPIC

There are multiple graduates, graduating from universities with lots of tuition debts and some even have to work part-time in high school. Others are lucky enough to have parents that tell them just enjoy their life for the moment and study. Do you think despite their upbringing and family's financial status, they should still find a part-time job? If so, what will that influence their future. Use specific examples and explain.

Write at least 250 words

Unit 16　許多畢業生大學畢業後都有學貸，有些甚至需要在高中兼職打工。你認為學生該享受當下還是儘管家庭財務狀況許可，仍要打工呢？這對他們的未來有什麼影響呢？請以具體實例解釋。

🎓 整合能力強化 ❶ 實際演練

請搭配左頁的題目和並構思和完成大作文的演練。

_____

_____

_____

_____

_____

_____

_____

_____

_____

_____

_____

_____

_____

_____

_____

_____

_____

在掌握文法句型後，學習者大多能拿到 7 分以上的寫作成績，英語句型多樣性是獲取高分的關鍵，現在請演練接下來的單句中譯英練習。請務必演練後再觀看答案，也可以搭配範文音檔強化對各句型的記憶。

❶ 在《第一份工作》，創辦人 E.,分享了他的經驗，他的父母告訴他「有我生命的餘生去工作，而現在我應該僅僅需要學習和享受生活」。

_____

_____

【參考答案】

In *First Jobs*, a founder, E., shares his experience that his parents told him that he "had the rest of my life to work, and I should just study and enjoy life now."

❷ 我認為像是 E.這樣的人是非常幸運能有那樣子的父母，而且我並不反對寵小孩的這個想法。

_____

_____

【參考答案】

I think people like E., are very lucky to have that kind of parents, and I am not against the idea of pampering kids.

282

❸ 這某些程度上幫助我看到了現實世界中的另一瞥。

_____

_____

【參考答案】

It somehow helps me see another glimpse of the real world.

❹ 有些小孩在年紀很輕的階段就必須要開始工作了，但是我並沒有把他們視為是不幸運的類型。

_____

_____

【參考答案】

There are some kids who have to start to work at a very early age, but I do not view them as the unlucky type.

❺ 有些事情是你需要探索的，而在你大學四年的兼職工作就是其中一項。

_____

_____

【參考答案】

There are things that you need to explore, and working part time during four years of undergraduate study is one of them.

❻ 你能夠在學術環境之外做些什麼。你能夠在兼職工作之餘，學習如何處理問題。你在壓力之下能夠展示出你的工作能力。

You can do something outside the academic environment. You can learn how to cope with problems during working part-time. You demonstrate your ability to work under pressure.

❼ 你最終可以了解到什麼類型的工作最適合你，而你不想要以什麼維生。你將會對於周遭的人和事情有全然不同的想法。

You eventually figure what works best for you, and what you do not want to do for a living. You will have a totally different perspective to things and people around you.

❽ 或許你過去總認為錢很好賺，而藉由做些藍領工作，你了解到要賺一分錢有多麼艱難。

Perhaps you used to think money is easily earned, and by doing some blue-collar jobs, you understand how hard it is to earn a cent.

許多畢業生大學畢業後都有學貸，有些甚至需要在高中兼職打工。你認為學生該享受當下還是儘管家庭財務狀況許可，仍要打工呢？這對他們的未來有什麼影響呢？請以具體實例解釋。

❾ 你最終了解到你父母是多麼努力工作來支持你和你的家庭。

_____

_____

【參考答案】

You ultimately know how hard your parents have to work to support you and the family.

❿ 這些事情都不是你在學校環境中可以學習的到的，而你必須要經由做去了解到，你正逐漸的轉變成一位感恩的人，而從做那樣的工作你了解到你未來的道路，你不想要從事哪些工作，例如藍領工作。

_____

_____

【參考答案】

This thing cannot be learned in the school setting, and you have to do it to realize that. you are gradually becoming a grateful person, and from doing that kind of job, you figure out your future path that you do not want to do jobs, such as blue-collar jobs.

TOPIC

There are multiple graduates, graduating from universities with lots of tuition debts and some even have to work part-time in high school. Others are lucky enough to have parents that tell them just enjoy their life for the moment and study. Do you think despite their upbringing and family's financial status, they should still find a part-time job? If so, what will that influence their future. Use specific examples and explain.

搭配的暢銷書

■ *First Jobs*《第一份工作》

Step 1　題目是詢問是否要兼差打工呢，儘管經濟上不需要去打工，而打工對於一個人的影響又是什麼呢？先由《第一份工作》，創辦人 E 的經驗提到了與正常小孩都需要打工的不同的看法，而且提到並不反對寵小孩的看法。（父母其實對於小孩的養育方式是各式各樣的。）

Step 2　　次段表達出「有些小孩在年紀很輕的階段就必須要開始工作了，但是我並沒有把他們視為是不幸運的類型。」，另外提到關於自我探索和必須在學術環境外，藉由兼職去了解自己想要什麼，不想要什麼，這點蠻重要的。

Step 3　　再來提到藍領工作，從事這樣的兼職工作更能體會到父母的辛苦並且知道要感恩。

Step 4　　最後提到心境的轉換，這是遠超乎自己想像的，尤其是對人處事。另一部分是，都沒有打工經驗，讓面試官對你產生質疑，而且在面試過程中沒有經驗可以分享，例如克服挫折等的體驗。有打工經驗者則較具吸引力。最後總結出，這跟家庭背景等是無關的，打工對於畢業生求職是有幫助的。

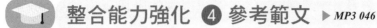

經由先前的演練後,現在請看整篇範文並聆聽音檔

In *First Jobs*, a founder, E., shares his experience that his parents told him that he "had the rest of my life to work, and I should just study and enjoy life now." I think people like E., are very lucky to have that kind of parents, and I am not against the idea of pampering kids. It somehow helps me see another glimpse of the real world.

在《第一份工作》,創辦人 E.,分享了他的經驗,他的父母告訴他「有我生命的餘生去工作,而現在我應該僅僅需要學習和享受生活」。我認為像是 E.這樣的人是非常幸運能有那樣子的父母,而且我並不反對寵小孩的這個想法。這某些程度上幫助我看到了現實世界中的另一瞥。

There are some kids who have to start to work at a very early age, but I do not view them as the unlucky type. There are things that you need to explore, and working part time during four years of undergraduate study is one of them. You can do something outside the academic environment. You can learn how to cope with problems during working part-time. You demonstrate your ability to work under pressure. You eventually figure what works best for you, and what you do not want to do for a living. You will have a totally different perspective to things and people around you.

有些小孩在年紀很輕的階段就必須要開始工作了，但是我並沒有把他們視為是不幸運的類型。有些事情是你需要探索的，而在你大學四年的兼職工作就是其中一項。你能夠在學術環境之外做些什麼。你能夠在兼職工作之餘，學習如何處理問題。你在壓力之下能夠展示出你的工作能力。你最終可以了解到什麼類型的工作最適合你，而你不想要以什麼維生。你將會對於周遭的人和事情有全然不同的想法。

Perhaps you used to think money is easily earned, and by doing some blue-collar jobs, you understand how hard it is to earn a cent. You ultimately know how hard your parents have to work to support you and the family. This thing cannot be learned in the school setting, and you have to do it to realize that. You are gradually becoming a grateful person, and from doing that kind of job, you figure out your future path that you do not want to do jobs, such as blue-collar jobs.

或許你過去總認為錢很好賺，而藉由做些藍領工作，你了解到要賺一分錢有多麼艱難。你最終了解到你父母是多麼努力工作來支持你和你的家庭。這些事情都不是你在學校環境中可以學習的到的，而你必須要經由做去了解到，你正逐漸的轉變成一位感恩的人，而從做那樣的工作你了解到你未來的道路，你不想要從事哪些工作，例如藍領工作。

The mind-shifting makes you a changed person. When you are back to school, you have become a more focused person. You really want to perfect your skills so that you will get an ideal white-collar job after you graduate. The repercussions are more than what you can think of. You treat things differently. All these cannot be done if you have not done any part-time job, and it is actually a plus when you are looking for a job. It can be a story for you to share whether it is something that you do not do well, but eventually learn how to do it well. Interviewers will take that kind of things to heart, but when you solely focus on the study and without these experiences, you have nothing to say during the job search. It really makes you less intriguing.

心境的轉換讓你成了個全然不同的人。當你回到學校之後，你已經成了一位更具專注的人。你真的想要完善你的技能，這樣一來你就能夠在你畢業後有理想的白領工作。這些影響是超乎你想像的。你對待事情的方式也不同了。如果你沒有做過任何兼職工作，所有這些都無法達成，實際上這對於你要找工作也是加分的。這可以成為是你能分享的故事，不論是一些你沒做好的事情，但是最終學習如何把它做好。面試官們會把這些聽進心頭裡，但當你僅專注於學習上，而沒有這些經驗時，你在找工作時就沒有東西可以分享。這讓你看起來較不具吸引力。

To sum up, I think it has nothing to do with the family's financial status and backgrounds. Doing a few part-time jobs helps graduates in the long term.

總之，我認為這與一個家庭的財務狀況和背景無關。長遠來說，從事幾份兼職工作對畢業生是有幫助的。

是否該協議薪資呢？還是接受資方所給予的薪資呢？

 Writing Task 2 ▶ *MP3 047*

TOPIC

Unemployment rates for graduates are high and salaries given by modern employers are low. Still people care about their earnings. Some say that you don't ask the number of your salary because you really need to get on the board. Others think despite the economic downturn it does not do any harm to negotiate the salary. What is the thinking behind the hiring? Use specific examples and explain.

Write at least 250 words

整合能力強化 ❶ 實際演練

請搭配左頁的題目和並構思和完成大作文的演練。

_____

_____

_____

_____

_____

_____

_____

_____

_____

_____

_____

_____

_____

_____

_____

_____

Part 1
雅思寫作 Task1：精選高分字彙

Part 2
雅思寫作 Task1：圖表題小作文

Part 3
雅思寫作 **Task2**：大作文

整合能力強化 ❷ 單句中譯英演練

　　英語句型多樣性是獲取高分的關鍵，現在請演練接下來的單句中譯英練習。請務必演練後再觀看答案，也可以搭配範文音檔強化對各句型的記憶。

❶ 縈繞在數百萬畢業生心中的最大的問題是薪資，尤其是第一份薪水。

_____

_____

【參考答案】

The biggest question that lingers the mind of millions of graduates is the salary, especially the first salary.

❷ 這確實是畢業生的困境，因為對於畢業生來說，失業率高而協商價格或薪資是具有風險的。

_____

_____

【參考答案】

It is really a dilemma for graduates because unemployment rates for graduates are high and negotiating the price or salary is risky.

❸ 相當可能的情況是，在有限的預算內，高階主管最終會錄用一些接受公司所提供薪資的面試者們，而非有些會跟公司協議薪資者。

【參考答案】

It is quite possible that within a limited amount of the budget, the executive who eventually makes the hiring decision recruits someone who accepts what the company offers to the interviewee, rather than someone who negotiates.

❹ 情況也可能有所不同。如果你讓他們印象極深刻，相當有可能高階主管最終會讓步，而你最終也能獲得你理想薪資的工作錄用通知。

【參考答案】

The scenario can also be very different. If you impress them enough, it is quite likely that the executive will eventually make room for it, and you eventually get the job offer with the desired salary.

❺ 對於畢業生來說，在缺乏協商技巧和與人打交道的技巧，要做那樣的事情和獲得雙贏的結果是相當艱難的。

【參考答案】

It is really hard for graduates without negotiating skills and people skills to do such a thing and get the win-win result.

❻ 在《我在工作中所犯的錯誤》，雅琳娜・圖貞德分享了她關於協議薪資的智慧，「即使當你對於第一份工作感到感恩，協議薪資仍是個不錯的想法」。

_____

_____

【參考答案】

In *"Mistakes I Made at Work"*, Alina Tugend shares her wisdom about negotiating the salary, "even when you're grateful to have that first job, it is still a good idea to negotiate."

❼ 我認為雅琳娜提供了非常好的洞察。你不用對自己限制那麼多，並將自己視成卑微的求職者。雙方都在評估彼此。

_____

_____

【參考答案】

I think Alina provides a very good insight. You do not have to limit yourself so much and treat yourself as the humble person looking for a job.

❽ 也就是，你也正評估這間公司，但你需要知道的是要維持冷靜，而且當在協議薪資時，不要表現得很魯莽。

_____

_____

【參考答案】

Both parties are evaluating each other. That is, you are evaluating the company as well, but you need to be calm and do not come across as rude when negotiating the salary.

❾ 你也需要知道的是，所有公司都是利益導向的，而且是人事專員和高階主管的工作去盡可能的降低薪資，所以這樣在老闆的眼裡，他們是替公司想的一群，而他們以較為低廉的價格雇用一些卓越的面試者，這件事是很棒的。

【參考答案】

You also need to know that all companies are profit-driven, and it is the HR personnel's or the executive's job to lower the salary as much as possible, so to the eyes of the boss, they are thinking about the company, and they are doing a great job hiring someone excellent by using a much lower price.

❿ 如果你接受了初次的供價，那麼相當可能的是，其他與你有相同學歷和證照的候選人，但有提出議價者，得到了比你更高的薪資，可能多 2 到 3 千元。

【參考答案】

If you accept the first offer, then it is quite possible that other candidates who have the same degree and certificates as you, but negotiate the salary will get a much higher salary than you, perhaps NT 2,000 or 3,000 more.

整合能力強化 ❸ 段落拓展

TOPIC

Unemployment rates for graduates are high and salaries given by modern employers are low. Still people care about their earnings. Some say that you don't ask the number of your salary because you really need to get on the board. Others think despite the economic downturn it does not do any harm to negotiate the salary. What is the thinking behind the hiring? Use specific examples and explain.

搭配的暢銷書

■ *Mistakes I Made at Work*《我在工作中所犯的錯誤》

Step 1   首段先定義出薪資對於畢業生的重要性。

■ 但是 ❶ 失業率高也是影響畢業生是否會跟雇主協議薪資，因為大多數的畢業生，還是會抱持「先求有再求好」的心態。

■ ❷ 協議更高的薪資確實讓畢業生面臨不被雇用的風險，因為通常公司很可能選擇第一次就接受公司所給予的薪資的面試者。

■ ❸ 畢業生缺乏協商技巧和與人打交道的技巧，這很可能讓畢業生搞砸了一次機會。

Step 2　次段提到了跟首段不太一樣的想法，在《我在工作中所犯的錯誤》，雅琳娜提出了另一個看法，抱持感恩但仍需要協議薪資。這其實是蠻正確的想法，而且你確實必須替自己做些什麼，當你對薪資沒意見時，等同你對薪資是同意的。接著表達出必須要拋開限制但不魯莽的替自己爭取符合自己更好的待遇。另外要知道的是，公司方面其實都是盡可能的降低薪資，想購買東西一樣，大家都希望用最少的錢購買到最好的商品。

Step 3　最後一段提到一個關鍵，公司方面並不希望你察覺到這點。然後提到了一個薪資範圍，其實公司對於每個職位都有薪資的核定，而在談判薪資時，通常會有一個範圍，跟面試者會在資料表上寫一個範圍是一樣的，公司可能會先詢問是否接受某個薪資，而不太可能是那個範圍內最高的值，因為懂得協商者會先拉高想要的薪資，畢竟公司會在砍一些，然後面試者也能獲取近似自己本來理想薪資的待遇。另一個還要知道的部分是，同樣學經歷，有提跟沒有提其實還是有差別的，文中有舉例，現實中也常發生沒替自己爭取的例子，但後來後悔的情況，最後總結出，還是要替自己爭取，即使最後得到的待遇並沒有增加。

經由先前的演練後，現在請看整篇範文並聆聽音檔

The biggest question that lingers the mind of millions of graduates is the salary, especially the first salary. It is really a dilemma for graduates because unemployment rates for graduates are high and negotiating the price or salary is risky. It is quite possible that within a limited amount of the budget, the executive who eventually makes the hiring decision recruits someone who accepts what the company offers to the interviewee, rather than someone who negotiates. The scenario can also be very different. If you impress them enough, it is quite likely that the executive will eventually make room for it, and you eventually get the job offer with the desired salary. It is really hard for graduates without negotiating skills and people skills to do such a thing and get the win-win result.

縈繞在數百萬畢業生心中的最大的問題是薪資，尤其是第一份薪水。這確實是畢業生的困境，因為對於畢業生來說，失業率高而協商價格或薪資是具有風險的。相當可能的情況是，在有限的預算內，高階主管最終會錄用一些接受公司所提供薪資的面試者們，而非有些會跟公司協議薪資者。情況也可能有所不同。如果你讓他們印象極深刻，相當有可能高階主管最終會讓步，而你最終也能獲得你理想薪資的工作錄用通知。對於畢業生來說，在缺乏協商技巧和與人打交道的技巧，要做那樣的事情和獲得雙贏的結果是相當艱難的。

In *"Mistakes I Made at Work"*, Alina Tugend shares her wisdom about negotiating the salary, "even when you're grateful to have that first job, it is still a good idea to negotiate." I think Alina provides a very good insight. You do not have to limit yourself so much and treat yourself as the humble person looking for a job. Both parties are evaluating each other. That is, you are evaluating the company as well, but you need to be calm and do not come across as rude when negotiating the salary. You also need to know that all companies are profit-driven, and it is the HR personnel's or the executive's job to lower the salary as much as possible, so to the eyes of the boss, they are thinking about the company, and they are doing a great job hiring someone excellent by using a much lower price.

301

在《我在工作中所犯的錯誤》，雅琳娜・圖貞德分享了她關於協議薪資的智慧，「即使當你對於第一份工作感到感恩，協議薪資仍是個不錯的想法」。我認為雅琳娜提供了非常好的洞察。你不用對自己限制那麼多，並將自己視成卑微的求職者。雙方都在評估彼此。也就是，你也正評估這間公司，但你需要知道的是要維持冷靜，而且當在協議薪資時，不要表現得很魯莽。你也需要知道的是，所有公司都是利益導向的，而且是人事專員和高階主管的工作去盡可能的降低薪資，所以這樣在老闆的眼裡，他們是替公司想的一群，而他們以較為低廉的價格雇用一些卓越的面試者，這件事是很棒的。

Of course, they do not want you to notice that, and they want you to accept their first offer. The first offering price is often the lowest range in their budget because they know experienced job applicants will negotiate the price. If they are offering you NT 27,000 dollars, the range could be NT 27,000 to NT 32,000 dollars. If you accept the first offer, then it is quite possible that other candidates who have the same degree and certificates as you, but negotiate the salary will get a much higher salary than you, perhaps NT 2,000 or 3,000 more. It is also quite likely that after a year, you accidentally know that and lamented that you agreed and did not negotiate to do anything for yourself back then. To sum up, I think you should do your homework about the position you are applying for and really know what other companies offer the salary for a position like this, and it does hurt to negotiate the price, but do not offend the interviewer or go insanely high.

當然，他們不想要你察覺到這些，且他們想要你接受他們的初次供價。第一次的供價通常是他們預算裡頭最低範圍的，因為他們知道有經驗的工作申請者將會協議價格。如果他們提供你台幣 2 萬 7 千元的薪資，這個範圍可能介於 2 萬 7 千元到 3 萬 2 千元。如果你接受了初次的供價，那麼相當可能的是，其他與你有相同學歷和證照的候選人，但有提出議價者，得到了比你更高的薪資，可能多 2 到 3 千元。相當有可能，經過一年工作後，你無意中知道且悲嘆你當初居然在第一次就接受對方提出的薪資，而且沒有議價或在當時替自己做些什麼。總之，我認為你應該要做好功課，關於你正申請的職位，並且真的知道其他公司所提供像這樣性質的職務，所給的薪資為何，而雖然協議價格確實很傷，但是別觸怒了面試官或是提瘋狂高的價格。

303

UNIT 18

你對於「公司給多少錢做多少事」或「沒獎勵就不把事情做好」的看法是什麼呢？

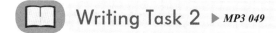

Writing Task 2 ▶ *MP3 049*

TOPIC

People have a various idea about work, and first jobs are often not that great. Some claim that they should only put the effort based on how the employer gives them in return. Others have a totally different perspective, thinking they should do it 100% in the workplace no matter how they are treated in the workplace. What is your opinion about this? Use specific examples and explain.

Write at least 250 words

🎓 整合能力強化 ❶ 實際演練

請搭配左頁的題目和並構思和完成大作文的演練。

Part 1
雅思寫作 Task1：精選高分字彙

Part 2
雅思寫作 Task1：圖表題小作文

Part 3
雅思寫作 Task2：大作文

在掌握文法句型後，學習者大多能拿到 7 分以上的寫作成績，英語句型多樣性是獲取高分的關鍵，現在請演練接下來的單句中譯英練習。請務必演練後再觀看答案，也可以搭配範文音檔強化對各句型的記憶。

❶ 儘管不是關於你在這份工作中付出多多的時間，你會藉由做中學，而大部分是在公司資深工作者的智慧。

_____

_____

【參考答案】

Although it is not about the length of time you put yourself in the work, you will learn something by doing, and mostly wisdom from senior workers in the company.

❷ 新聘人員可能會認為，為什麼不能，我基於公司給予我多少薪資和獎金，付出多少的努力。

_____

_____

【參考答案】

Newly recruits might think, why not, I'm putting in the effort based on the salary and bonuses the company gives me.

❸ 對已經找到第一份工作的數百萬畢業生，他們正在工作的公司無
法提供這些。第一份工作通常不是那麼棒，而這樣想也沒有什麼
不對之處。

【參考答案】

For millions of graduates who have found their first job, the
companies they are currently working cannot provide that. First
jobs are usually not that great, and there is nothing wrong to think
that way.

❹ 你根據老闆所給你的，而付出多少在工作上，但是還是有其他洞
察讓你能好好思考下。

【參考答案】

You do the work on the basis of what the boss gives to you, but
there are other insights for you to think about.

❺ 在《我在工作中所犯的錯誤》，蘿拉·圖比分享了她在工作中的
智慧，「取而代之的是，你幾乎需要將自己視為是自由工作者，
建立技巧和能力，讓你能帶到下份工作和下下份工作」。

Part 1
雅思寫作 Task1：精選高分字彙

Part 2
雅思寫作 Task1：圖表題小作文

Part 3
雅思寫作 Task2：大作文

307

In *"Mistakes I Made at Work"*, Laurel Touby shares her wisdom about work, "Instead, you almost need to see yourself as a freelancer, building skills and capabilities to take with you to the next job and the next job."

❻ 我認為蘿拉在態度上很正確,而大多數的新僱人員能夠看事情時也朝這方向思考。你必須要意識到你的下份工作是基於你現在這份工作的表現。

I think Laurel is right about the attitude, and most newly recruits just cannot see things in that kind of direction. You have to realize that your next job is based on the job you are currently doing.

❼ 你在現在這份工作上做得多好影響到你在現在能拿到多少的薪資和獎金回報,以及下份工作,所以付出 100%,即使你對於你現在的工作並不滿意。

How well you do your current job affects the return you are going to get in the salary, bonus, and the next job, so do it 100% even if you are unsatisfied with your current job.

❽ 有些人轉職而獲取了理想的薪資或職位，因為他們在前一份的工作上有好的表現。

_____

_____

【參考答案】

Some people who make a job hop and who get the desired salary or position are because how well they are doing in the previous job.

❾ 如果你在現在這份工作上沒有好的表現，那究竟為什麼獵人頭公司想要僱用你，並給你較高的獎勵等等的。你必須要看長期，而非短期。

_____

_____

【參考答案】

If you do not do well in the current job, why on earth that a job hunter wants to recruit you and give you a better benefit and so on. You have to look for the long-term, not the short-term.

❿ 隨著經濟蕭條，任何事情都很有可能發生。很可能當你走進辦公室時，你從公告中得知公司於一周內即將關閉。

_____

_____

【參考答案】

It is highly likely that when you walk into the office and you get the announcement that the company is going to close in a week.

TOPIC

People have a various idea about work, and first jobs are often not that great. Some claim that they should only put the effort based on how the employer gives them in return. Others have a totally different perspective, thinking they should do it 100% in the workplace no matter how they are treated in the workplace. What is your opinion about this? Use specific examples and explain.

搭配的暢銷書

■ *Mistakes I Made at Work*《我在工作中所犯的錯誤》

Step 1 　首段先定義工作，剛畢業的大學生或新聘人員，對於工作的想法會跟工作幾年後的資深人員有差異，這是不同的領會。

Step 2 　次段進一步表明了新聘人員的想法，表達出這樣的想法其實沒有任何不對之處，是很合於情理的，你拿到多少就付出多少。

Step 3　下個段落則談到值得令人深省的部分，在《我在工作中所犯的錯誤》，其中一位作者蘿拉提到了工作是關於建立技能等，這是很正確的態度（其實學到的東西都是你能帶走的，這些別人無法拿走，甚至在下份工作中會使用到）。

- 而且這關乎到接下來的陳述，包含 ❶ 下份工作和 ❷ 現在的工作，你的下份工作是基於你現在這份工作的表現，而且你現在工作中所能獲取的加薪和獎金也與你現有的工作表現有關。

- ❸ 轉職或跳槽時能有更好的談判籌碼也跟你現在的表現有關。

- 最後陳述出要以長遠的方向去思考。

Step 4　最後總結，提到蘿拉談到的部分，不能仰賴每任雇主，雇主不太可能終身聘用你，且有可能隨時關門，而為了避免失業後找不到工作，要必須不斷學習並且累積自己下份工作能用到的技能和經驗，這才是正確的態度，不斷計較或許老闆等都不覺得如何，但自己所累積的經驗和技能也相對有限，找新工作時，還是會輸給原先公司不計較且願意承擔更多責任的同事，長遠來說是吃虧的。

經由先前的演練後,現在請看整篇範文並聆聽音檔

To millions of graduates or newly recruits, it is quite possible they have a drastically different idea about work, compared with those who have worked for a few years. Although it is not about the length of time you put yourself in the work, you will learn something by doing, and mostly wisdom from senior workers in the company.

對於數百萬的畢業生或新聘人員,相當有可能他們對於工作有極大不同的想法,與過去已經工作幾年的那些人相比的話。儘管不是關於你在這份工作中付出多多的時間,你會藉由做中學,而大部分是在公司資深工作者的智慧。

Newly recruits might think, why not, I'm putting in the effort based on the salary and bonuses the company gives me. For millions of graduates who have found their first job, the companies they are currently working cannot provide that. First jobs are usually not that great, and there is nothing wrong to think that way. You do the work on the basis of what the boss has given to you, but there are other insights for you to think about.

新聘人員可能會認為，為什麼不能，我基於公司給予我多少薪資和獎金，付出多少的努力。對已經找到第一份工作的數百萬畢業生，他們正在工作的公司無法提供這些。第一份工作通常不是那麼棒，而這樣想也沒有什麼不對之處。你根據老闆所給你的，而付出多少在工作上，但是還是有其他洞察讓你能好好思考下。

In *"Mistakes I Made at Work"*, Laurel Touby shares her wisdom about work, "Instead, you almost need to see yourself as a freelancer, building skills and capabilities to take with you to the next job and the next job." I think Laurel is right about the attitude, and most newly recruits just cannot see things in that kind of direction. You have to realize that your next job is based on the job you are currently doing. How well you do your current job affects the return you are going to get in the salary, bonus, and the next job, so do it 100% even if you are unsatisfied with your current job. Some people who make a job hop and who get the desired salary or position are because how well they are doing in the previous job. If you do not do well in the current job, why on earth that a job hunter wants to recruit you and give you a better benefit and so on. You have to look for the long-term, not the short-term.

在《我在工作中所犯的錯誤》，蘿拉・圖比分享了她在工作中的智慧，「取而代之的是，你幾乎需要將自己視為是自由工作者，建立技巧和能力，讓你能帶到下份工作和下下份工作」。我認為蘿拉在態度上很正確，而大多數的新僱人員能夠看事情時也朝這方向思考。你必須要意識到，你的下份工作是基於你現在這份工作的表現。你在現在這份工作上做得多好影響到你在現在能拿到多少的薪資和獎金回報，以及下份工作，所以付出 100%，即使你對於你現在的工作並不滿意。有些人轉職而獲取了理想的薪資或職位，是因為他們在前一份的工作上有好的表現。如果你在現在這份工作上沒有好的表現，那究竟為什麼獵人頭公司想要雇用你，並給你較高的獎勵等等的。你必須要看長期，而非短期。

There are other vital points that Laurel mentions. You cannot rely on the bonus and many other things to do a job or a task well. You need to be internally motivated and you are doing it for yourself. With the economic downturn, it is quite possible that anything can happen. It is highly likely that when you walk into the office and you get the announcement that the company is going to close in a week. If you are not thinking about yourself and working hard, it is quite likely that you are going to end up being jobless and have no or enough experiences to find the next job. To sum up, I think whatever job you do or under what circumstances do it 100% so that you can take those experiences with you.

這些都是蘿拉提到的重要之處。你不可能仰賴獎金或許多其他的事情去做好工作或任務。你需要自己本身有足夠的動力驅策著你，而你是替你自己而做。隨著經濟蕭條，任何事情都很有可能發生。很可能當你走進辦公室時，你從公告中得知公司於一周內即將關閉。如果你沒有替自己思考且努力工作的話，很可能你最終會以失業結尾，而且沒有或有足夠的經驗找到下份工作。總之，我認為不論你所從事的工作為何，或是在任何情況下，都要付出 100%努力，這樣一來你就可以將經驗一起帶走。

雅思寫作引用和出處

寫作單元 /Part 3	參考書籍	引述句子
Unit 1	*Mistakes I Made at Work*	"Don't expect too much of yourself when you're young. It's better to be a late bloomer than an early one; so many young successes flame out and spend the rest of their lives lamenting what they used to have." (Jessica, 2014, p.170)
Unit 1	*Getting There*	"In Hollywood, there are two kinds of executives: The flames that burn brightly and quickly go out and the executives who have long, interesting, and powerful careers. I aspired to be one of the latter." (Gillian, 2015, p.174)
Unit 3	*The Millionaire Next Door*	"one earns to spend. When you need to spend more, you need to earn more". (Thomas and William, 1996, p.52)
Unit 3	*Rich Dad Poor Dad*	"more money won't solve the problem." (Robert, 1997, 2011, 2017, p.32)
Unit 3	*Rich Dad Poor Dad*	"money without financial intelligence is money soon gone." (Robert, 1997, 2011, 2017, p.64)
Unit 4	*The Defining Decade*	"Resumes are just lists, and lists are not compelling." (Meg, 2012, p.62)
Unit 4	*How Luck Happens*	"you are going to need luck to get a job." (Janice and Barnaby, 2018, p.173)
Unit 4	*The Success Equation*	"the six interviewers voted against hiring you" "the head guy overrode their assessment and insisted we bring you in." (Michael, 2012, p.2)

寫作單元 /Part 3	參考書籍	引述句子
Unit 5	*Getting There*	"Many students are so focused on getting the right grades, so they can get into the right school that it barely gives them the chance to try something zany." (Gillian, 2015, p.175)
Unit 5	*First Jobs*	"I had spent years to get there, but I didn't really ever decide this." (Merritt, 2015, p.146)
Unit 6	*How Will You Measure Your Life*	"The only way to be truly satisfied is to do what you believe is great work. And the only way to do great work is to love what you do." (Clayton, 2012, SECTION 1)
Unit 6	*Where You Go Is Not Who You Will Be*	"you'll figure out how to make money once you figure out what you love to do." (Frank, 2015, p.79)
Unit 7	*How Will You Measure Your Life*	"its leaders had deceptively co-opted her time and talents in the prime of her life." (Clayton, 2012, p.59)
Unit 8	*"The Promise of the Pencil : how an ordinary person can create an extraordinary change"*	"There actually will be times in life when you should choose money over experience." "but make that choice when the margin is much bigger, when the margin is millions of dollars, not thousand." (Adam, 2014, p.62-63)
Unit 9	*The Defining Decade*	"In fact, most of the people she compared herself to were older than she was or had been working longer than she had." (Meg, 2012, p.157)

寫作單元 /Part 3	參考書籍	引述句子
Unit 19	*Mistakes I Made at Work*	"don't expect too much of yourself when you are young." (Jessica, 2014, p.170)
Unit 10	*Mistakes I Made at Work*	"Procrastination will prevent you from fully living your life; instead learn to appreciate your mistakes." (Jessica, 2014, p.224)
Unit 10	*Originals*	"procrastination might be conducive to originality." (Adam, 2016, p.94)
Unit 10	*Originals*	"procrastination may be the enemy of productivity, but it can be a resource of creativity." (Adam, 2016, p.95)
Unit 11	*Rich Dad Poor Dad*	"Often in the real world, it's not the smart who get ahead, but the bold." (Robert, 1997, 2011, 2017, p.145)
Unit 11	*What I Wish I Knew When I was 20*	"The world is divided into people who wait for others to give them permission to do the things they want to do and people who grant themselves permission." (Tina, 2009, p.57)
Unit 11	*Rich Dad Poor Dad*	"Winners are not afraid of losing. But losers are." (Robert, 1997, 2011, 2017, p.166)
Unit 13	*The Defining Decade*	"For those who have a growth mindset, failures may sting but they are also viewed as opportunities for improvement and change." (Meg, 2012, p. 158)
Unit 13	*Mistakes I Made at Work*	"When you have a "growth mindset", you understand that mistakes and setbacks are an inevitable part of learning." (Jessica, 2014, p.250)

寫作單元 /Part 3	參考書籍	引述句子
Unit 14	*Mistakes I Made at Work*	"The idea of "work-life balance" is not necessarily helpful. If you are immersed in your work and raising a family, you might feel a lot of good things – but it may not include balanced." (Jessica, 2014, p.71)
Unit 14	*The Job*	"the more you talk about work-life balance, the more you create the problem that you want to solve." (Ellen, 2018, p.43)
Unit 15	*Business Model You*	"dream job is often created than found." (Tim, Alexander, and Yves, 2012, p.85)
Unit 15	*Rich Dad Poor Dad*	"The problem was that he couldn't find an equivalent job that recognized his seniority from the old company." (Robert, 1997, 2011, 2017, p.151)
Unit 16	*First Jobs*	"had the rest of my life to work, and I should just study and enjoy life now." (Merritt, 2015, p.213-214)
Unit 17	*Mistakes I Made at Work*	"even when you're grateful to have that first job, it is still a good idea to negotiate." (Jessica, 2014, p.114)
Unit 18	*Mistakes I Made at Work*	"Instead, you almost need to see yourself as a freelancer, building skills and capabilities to take with you to the next job and the next job." (Jessica, 2014, p.11)

國家圖書館出版品預行編目(CIP)資料

一次就考到雅思寫作7+/ 韋爾著-- 初版. --
新北市：倍斯特, 2019.09 面； 公分. --
（考用英語系列；20）
ISBN 978-986-98079-0-6（平裝附光碟）
1.國際英語語文測試系統　2.寫作法

805.189　　　　　　　　　108013917

考用英語系列 020

一次就考到雅思寫作7⁺（附英式發音MP3）

初　　　版　　2019年9月
定　　　價　　新台幣499元

作　　　者　　韋爾
出　　　版　　倍斯特出版事業有限公司
發 行 人　　周瑞德
電　　　話　　886-2-8245-6905
傳　　　真　　886-2-2245-6398
地　　　址　　23558 新北市中和區立業路83巷7號4樓
E - m a i l　　best.books.service@gmail.com
官　　　網　　www.bestbookstw.com
總 編 輯　　齊心瑀
特約編輯　　洪婉婷
封面構成　　高鍾琪
內頁構成　　菩薩蠻數位文化有限公司
印　　　製　　大亞彩色印刷製版股份有限公司

港澳地區總經銷　　泛華發行代理有限公司
地　　　址　　香港新界將軍澳工業邨駿昌街7號2樓
電　　　話　　852-2798-2323
傳　　　真　　852-3181-3973